"What do you say, Jill?"

Dan flashed her a disarming smile. "Will you let me help you for old time's sake?"

"If I do agree to let you help me," she said cautiously, "and I'm not saying I will—we work together. I'm not going to be shoved aside because some hotshot detective has entered the picture."

"Fair enough. I'll probably need an assistant, anyway."

She laughed. "In your dreams, Santini. This is an equal partnership. I'd like to make something clear, though. There will be no strings attached to this deal."

"Of course not." He smiled.

"After it's all over, we both go our separate ways."

"I wouldn't have it any other way."

Jill looked at him for a long measuring second. "In that case...we have a deal."

"Christiane Heggan delivers a tale that will leave you breathless."

—*Literary Times*

CHRISTIANE
HEGGAN

DeCeptiOn

MIRA®

ISBN 1-55166-466-6

DECEPTION

Copyright © 1998 by Christiane Heggan.

Printed in U.S.A.

To the two newest men in my life,
Zak and Alek,
with all my love

And to Bob, who makes everything perfect

Since a novel is never the work of just one person, I would like to thank the following people:

David W. Doelp, senior project architect, Kling Lindquist, for answering my many questions with patience, understanding and great wit. Any errors made or liberties taken in the interest of fiction are my own.

Rosemary Rys, Director, Corporate Communications, Kling Lindquist, for giving me the grand tour and supplying me with tons of information.

Bridget McQuate, Communications Director, AIA Philadelphia, for her marvelous profiling of some of today's most talented women architects.

Robert G. Martin of Bell Atlantic Properties, for an exciting and comprehensive tour of one of Philadelphia's most impressive skyscrapers.

Bob Clarke of Livingston Manor, New York, for sharing his thoughts and knowledge of this beautiful area of the Catskill Mountains.

And last but not least, a million *merci*s to my editors, Dianne Moggy, Amy Moore and Laura Shin for their unparalleled support and enthusiasm.

Prologue

A pelting rain struck the asphalt, turning the narrow mountain road slick and dangerous. Moving too fast for the conditions, a Jeep spun around a bend, pulled up in front of a dark-colored sedan parked alongside a deep ravine and skidded to a stop.

A man in a blue ski jacket jumped out of the Jeep. Rain beat on his head and shoulders as he hurried toward the sedan. Reaching inside, he flicked on the high beams and ran back to the Jeep.

Not a movement was wasted as he opened the rear hatch, reached inside, pulled out a limp body and dragged it to the driver's side, grunting with each step.

He didn't stop to catch his breath, though he needed it badly. Instead, he hoisted the body behind the wheel, struggling to keep the dead weight propped up while he strapped the seat belt in place. When he was done, the man reached for the gearshift and slid it into drive. Then, straightening, he slammed the door shut.

Angled against a steep slope, the Jeep immediately began to slip toward the ravine, slowly at first, then faster as it picked up momentum. Following a straight path, the car hurtled through the guardrail, leaped over the stony bank and plunged, nose first, into the deep valley below.

The sound of the crash, though expected, made the man flinch. For a moment, he stood frozen, oblivious of the rain, which ran down his face and pooled at his feet. Except for his heavy breathing and the look of sheer hatred in his eyes, he might have been as dead as the man he had just disposed of so neatly.

As the car exploded and a huge fiery ball soared toward the dark, stormy sky, he closed his eyes as if in prayer. ''You son of a bitch,'' he hissed between clenched teeth. ''I hope to God you burn in hell.''

Looking relieved, as if a great weight had been lifted off his shoulders, he turned away from the edge, ran back to the sedan and jumped behind the wheel. He had just strapped his own seat belt when a second, louder explosion rocked the night. As calmly as if he had just finished a round of golf, the man put the car in gear and slowly drove down the winding, treacherous road.

One

Standing in front of his bathroom mirror with a towel knotted around his hips and one half of his face covered with lather, Dan Santini cut through the thick foam with an expert hand while mentally running through the tests he would be handing to his students an hour from now.

Because his class was relatively small, he had allowed its members to stretch their preparation time until today, which meant that he had only one day to grade the tests and post the results before winter break.

Though a few would claim the extra day still wasn't enough, Dan had no doubt they would do fine. His was an exceptionally bright group, ten young men and women who showed great promise and made him proud to be their professor.

It was three years ago this month that he had begun his teaching career at Glenwood College in Oak Park, a small Chicago suburb ten miles north of the city. At first he'd had doubts as to whether he was cut out to be a professor, to teach rather than practice. But after only a few days, he had realized that his students not only valued his frank discussions but respected his opposing views. The give-and-take was energizing for everyone on either side of the classroom desk.

He didn't even miss New York. Or the force. No, that wasn't quite true, Dan thought as he lifted his chin and let the blade glide along his neck. There were times when he missed his job as a homicide detective, missed the methodic process of gathering clues, leading the hunt and questioning a suspect.

Especially questioning a suspect. Few things in life were more fascinating, more challenging than the human mind and its behavior when under pressure. It was because of his passion for exploring the many varieties of deviant criminal behavior that he had agreed to teach this particular course.

Applied criminal psychology was a catchall term for anything that dealt with the criminal mind. It was a subject Dan had studied and practiced for nearly all of the ten years he had worked as an NYPD homicide detective. But it wasn't until the arrest of one of New York City's most notorious serial killers in 1993 that Dan had emerged, much to his dismay, as something of an overnight celebrity because of it.

Gossip at the precinct had held to the view that he would make lieutenant within a few years, a prediction that was never tested. In 1994, during a murder investigation in a lower Manhattan tenement, the suspect Dan and his partner had been tracking had suddenly sprang out of nowhere, an Uzi in his hand, and begun spraying the room, seriously injuring two police officers. He had just turned on a third when Dan shot him. When the bloodbath was over, Dan had learned the age of the dead boy—fourteen.

For weeks afterward, the thought that he had killed a child had played heavily on Dan's conscience. That

Eddy Delgado was a street punk with a mean temper and a rap sheet a mile long had done little to alleviate the guilt Dan felt at this senseless loss of a young life.

Two months later, in spite of his superiors' protests, he had resigned from the force and begun looking for another job. A Brooklyner born and bred, leaving New York and his family hadn't been part of his plans. But when the president of Glenwood College, impressed by Dan's police experience and his master's degree in psychology, asked him to come to Chicago for an interview, Dan saw the request as a chance to make a truly clean start.

By the end of the day, he had been offered an associate professorship, a handsome salary and a chance to teach a course Dan knew and loved better than anything else—applied criminal psychology.

He had never regretted his decision.

His task finished, Dan ran water over his face and patted it dry. He was pouring a few drops of aftershave into his cupped palm, when the phone rang. He smiled. Only one person ever called him this early—his mother.

He was right, but instead of the cheerful hello he was accustomed to, Angelina Santini greeted him soberly. "Oh, Danny," she said with a catch in her voice. "Did you hear about Simon Bennett?"

Dan hadn't heard from his former father-in-law in years. "No. Something happened to him?"

"He's dead, Danny. He was on his way home from the Catskill Mountains and his Jeep went off the road. They say he was killed instantly."

Stunned, Dan shook his head as if to deny what he

had just heard. Not Simon. It couldn't be. The man was virtually indestructible. "When did this happen?" he asked.

"A few days ago. I would have called you sooner, but I didn't find out until just now. Joe and Maria were in Ohio all last week, visiting Maria's mother, and I was so busy taking care of the boys, I didn't pay much attention to the news."

Dan felt a sudden sinking feeling in his stomach. Jill. She must be devastated. She had adored her father.

"I'm going to call Jill a little later," his mother continued. She paused. "I'm sure she'd love to hear from you, too, Danny."

Dan knew better than to argue with his mother, especially on the subject of Jill Bennett. "I'll call her, Ma."

After he hung up, Dan stood looking at the phone. He and his ex-wife hadn't spoken a word to each other since their divorce in June 1985. He was probably the last person she wanted to hear from right now, yet he couldn't let Simon's death pass without some sort of acknowledgment.

From memory, he dialed the number of Jill's loft, the same loft they had shared years ago. At the fourth ring, the answering machine clicked on and Jill's cheerful voice came through, causing something deep within him to stir.

"Hi there. Sorry I can't take your call, but you know the drill, so do your thing and I'll get back to you ASAP. Bye."

Not waiting for the beep, Dan hung up. Those damn

machines. He never knew what to say into them, especially at a time like this. He'd wait a day or two and call back. Or better yet, he would send Jill a card. That would eliminate the very definite possibility of her hanging up on him.

Because, deep down, he was still a cop, Dan picked up the address book he always kept near the phone and flipped through the pages. Maybe Wally would be able to give him details of the accident. Wally Becker was the police constable of Livingston Manor, where the Bennetts owned their Catskills summer home, and a close friend of the family. Dan had met him thirteen years ago, the day he'd married Jill, and the two men, bound by their career as law enforcement officers, had formed an instant friendship.

Wally answered on the first ring. As usual his tone was gruff. "Becker."

"Wally. It's Dan Santini."

The constable's tone turned immediately friendly. "Dan, you old son of a gun. How have you been?"

"Richer now that a certain cheating buddy of mine no longer cleans me out at poker."

There was a low chuckle at the other end of the line. "Cheat, my ass. I always won fair and square. You were just a sore loser."

The two men were quiet for a moment. When Dan broke the silence, his voice was grave. "I just heard about Simon."

Wally made a sound with his tongue. "Terrible thing, isn't it? One moment the man is full of life, and the next he's at the bottom of a cliff, burned beyond recognition."

"You're sure it was him?"

"The dental records confirmed it."

"What happened, Wally? Simon could have driven that road in his sleep."

Dan heard the older man expel a long breath and could picture him running his hand through his coarse gray hair. "Bad weather on December 1 is mostly to blame, I'm afraid. That and the fact that Simon was drinking rather heavily that night."

"Doesn't sound like Simon. He loved his scotch but he never mixed it with driving."

"He did that night. We found evidence of it at the house."

"You're satisfied the crash was an accident, then?"

"Not you, too," Wally muttered in disgust.

Dan's antennae popped up. "Someone else suspects foul play?"

"Jill. She thinks her father may have been murdered."

At the mention of Jill's name, Dan felt that same old pull inside his chest. He tried to ignore it. "Why is that?"

"She says that a few days before his death, Simon was preoccupied, even nervous. When she questioned him about it, he brushed her concerns aside and told her she was imagining things. Then a couple of days after he died, she was going through his desk and found a request for a handgun permit."

"You investigated the death?"

"My deputy and I went over the crash scene inch by inch, and found nothing to sustain Jill's suspicions. I even sent a forensics team to the house. There was no evidence of foul play there, either. So, to answer your question, yes, I'm satisfied Simon's death was accidental. Six years ago there was another crash at that exact spot. We put in additional signs, warning of the hazard, but…'' He heaved a deep sigh and let his sentence trail unfinished.

Knowing Simon as well as he did, Dan found it difficult to accept the accident theory. His ex-father-in-law was an excellent driver, and a cautious one. In bad weather as well as in good, he would have paid particular attention to that stretch of road.

"What was Simon doing in the Catskills at this time of year, anyway? He doesn't ski, does he?"

"No, but it was an unusually mild and dry week-end—until Sunday night. He probably wanted to make one more trip before the winter season. You know how he loved it up here."

Dan knew perfectly. A fishing and hunting enthusiast, Simon had come upon the large tract of land by accident and had bought it within the week, claiming it was the most perfect place on earth.

Dan finally forced out the question that bothered him most.

"How's Jill holding up?"

"Her father's death hit her hard," Wally replied. "But you know what a trouper she is. I can't say the same for Amanda, though. She and Simon had just celebrated their thirty-sixth wedding anniversary." Wally paused. "Talking of Jill, have you called her yet?" His tone was light and casual, as if the question was the most natural in the world.

Not sure why, Dan didn't tell Wally about his earlier phone call. "No."

"You're going to, aren't you?"

Dan smiled. Professionally, Wally Becker was known as a tough guy, but deep down he was soft as a roasted marshmallow. And a born matchmaker. Like Simon, he had done his damnedest to keep Jill and Dan from divorcing twelve years ago. Dan wouldn't put it past him to try a little matchmaking now.

Taking his silence as a positive sign, Wally forged ahead. "The girl sure could use a little TLC right about now."

"I was never very good in that department, Wally. You know that."

"If you say so." Wally sounded disappointed.

After another minute or so of friendly chitchat and the promise to get together the next time Dan went to New York to visit his family, the two men said goodbye and hung up.

For a long time afterward, Dan stood looking out the window. Chicago at sunrise was a sight he never seemed to tire of—the endless shimmering lake to the east, the city's towering skyscape to the north and the bustling University of Chicago to the west. Today, however, the view left him indifferent. His thoughts were of Simon Bennett. During the short time Dan had known him, the man had been like a father to him, kind, understanding and supportive. After the divorce, the two men had even stayed in touch for a while, calling each other on the phone occasionally until, finally, they had drifted apart. But Dan had never forgotten him.

What if Jill's instincts were right? he wondered as he watched the December sun turn the lake surface a brilliant shade of gold. What if Simon had been the victim of foul play?

He sighed. *Not your problem, old boy. Not anymore.*

After a while, he left the window and went to the bedroom to dress.

For reasons he wouldn't even try to explain, he was unable to get Jill out of his mind for the rest of the day.

Jill Bennett sat in Wally Becker's office in Livingston Manor Town Hall, trying hard not to remember the last time she was here—with her father. Ten days had gone by since his death and though the fierce pain had turned into a dull ache, at times the void he had left was almost unbearable.

For the first twenty-four hours after the accident, she hadn't wanted to believe he was gone, that she would never again see that familiar wink or hear his hearty laugh. It wasn't until the memorial service that the stark reality of her father's death had finally hit her.

She still had nightmares about the way he'd died. In the unconsciousness of sleep, images would flash— her father's Jeep skidding on the wet surface, flying over the edge, bouncing against the rocks, exploding.

She shook her head as if to chase the disturbing images and watched Wally pull out a file from a drawer. He was a short, stocky man with craggy features and a bushy mustache that had turned the same pewter gray as his hair. He'd been a friend of the family ever since her father had built the summer house twenty-one years ago.

"Here it is, Jill. A detailed report of my investigation." Wally dropped the file in front of her. "I know it's not what you were hoping for, but I'll stand by what I said at the memorial service last week. Your father's death was an accident, a terrible, senseless accident."

"But it can't be." Jill's voice was tight with emotion. "My father was too good a driver, and he knew that road too well to have had such an accident."

Wally leaned back in his chair and stifled a sigh. "It was very late. He was probably tired."

"Did you talk to the mechanic?" she asked stubbornly. "Inspect the car?"

Wally nodded. "There wasn't much to look at, but Marcus is positive the brake lines weren't cut. If they had been, the master cylinder would have been empty. And it wasn't. There was plenty of brake fluid left."

"What about the house? Whose fingerprints did you find?" Jill felt silly questioning an experienced policeman like Wally as if he were a novice, but she knew he hadn't taken her suspicions seriously when she had first approached him last week, and she had to be sure nothing had been overlooked.

"All we found were Simon's prints and those of nearly every member of your family, which isn't surprising since you all spent the Thanksgiving weekend up here."

Despite her determination to be strong, Jill's eyes welled up with tears. What a wonderful three days that had been. On Thanksgiving Day her mother had cooked a gigantic turkey, nearly burning it to a crisp. After dinner, her uncle Cyrus had sat at the piano and played a medley of Christmas carols. Within moments, the whole family was singing, most of them terribly off-key. Even her cousin Olivia, always such a bitch at family gatherings, had been almost pleasant that day.

"We also found spilled liquor next to his glass," Wally said gravely. "And on the floor."

Jill frowned. "What are you saying?"

"I'm saying that your father may have been drinking a little more than usual that night, and that his motor reflexes weren't as sharp as they should have been. To that you add the late hour, and the heavy rain." He shook his head. "That's a terrible combination, Jill."

"But that, too, doesn't make sense, Wally." Jill leaned forward, every nerve taut. "My father never drank before a road trip. Especially in bad weather."

"But he *was* drinking, honey. And it's *his* fingerprints we found on the glass, and on the bottle, not anyone else's. You said yourself he was troubled those last few days. Maybe whatever was bothering him drove him to drink, to do all the irrational things he wouldn't normally do."

As Jill's shoulders sagged in frustration, Wally nodded at the file on his desk. "Why don't you take a look at my report, Jill. It'll only take a few minutes. And maybe after you've read it, everything will make more sense to you."

His index finger curled around his mouth, Wally watched her leaf through the detailed six-page report he had compiled since Simon Bennett's death ten days ago. Just sitting there looking at her, he could see why his new deputy had turned into a bumbling fool at his first sight of her.

Although Jill was a Bennett in many ways, her good looks came from her mother, Amanda. Not as classically beautiful as Amanda, Jill nonetheless had the same proud carriage, the same wide, mobile mouth, the same thick, glossy auburn hair. Only the eyes, a deep marine blue like her father's, identified her as a Bennett.

But while Amanda was very conscious of her beauty and always strived to enhance it, Jill had a total disregard for her own. Even the way she dressed had a healthy, girl-next-door quality to it that belied her social status. He was glad to see that, unlike Amanda, she had abided by her father's wishes not to wear black after his death. Today's outfit was a riot of autumn colors that suited her perfectly—slim brown pants tucked into knee-high boots, a bright yellow sweater and a rust-colored suede jacket. Wally didn't know much about fashion but he knew style when he saw it.

A graduate of Columbia School of Architecture, Jill had incorporated that very style into her work by blending modern and traditional architecture in a unique way. Her first major commission, the new Symphony House in Tucson, Arizona, three years ago, had firmly established her as one of the country's most talented young architects. A reporter for *Architectural Record* once wrote that while Simon Bennett was the genius behind Bennett & Associates, Jill was its heart and soul.

She was tough. She'd had to be to compete in a profession that was still largely dominated by men, yet there was a vulnerability about her that was touching and refreshing. Wally had never been more conscious of that vulnerability than when Jill's divorce had become final. The poor kid had fallen apart, and it had taken months for Simon and the rest of the family to get her through the ordeal.

When Jill was finished reading the report, she snapped the folder shut. "Thanks, Wally. I truly appreciate the time you and your deputy spent on this."

She gave Wally a brave smile, and for a moment he almost believed that she had accepted the inevitable conclusion that her father's death was an accident. But something about the way she held his gaze told him she wasn't about to give up so easily. The girl might be appeased but she wasn't convinced. And that scared the hell out of him. A widower with no children, Wally had developed a deep affection for Jill and hated to see her consumed by this need to investigate Simon's death.

"Let it go, Jill," he said, knowing damn well she wouldn't. "Allow yourself to grieve and then go on with your life. That's what your father would have wanted."

Jill didn't answer. Suddenly restless, she stood up and walked over to the window. It was only mid-December, but in the Catskill Mountains winter had arrived. A light dusting of snow coated the parking lot, and in the distance the roaring sound of Sno-Cats could be heard as they groomed the rolling hills.

Her gaze swept across the snowcapped mountains her father had loved so much. With a pinch in her heart, she remembered that this was the year he'd wanted to learn how to ski.

"And you're going to teach me," he had told Jill one morning during one of their frequent mountain hikes.

Although thrilled at the idea, she hadn't been able to resist a little harmless teasing. "You want to do *what* at your age?" she had exclaimed in mock horror. "Are you sure those old bones can take it?"

He had laughed with her. "I'll show you what these old bones can do."

Feeling the familiar prickle behind her eyelids, Jill bit her lip to stop the tears that threatened to erupt. She had done enough crying in the last ten days. From now on, her energy would have to be focused on something a little more constructive. Like finding out what had truly happened to her father. And if he had been murdered, as she was beginning to suspect, then she would extend her efforts one step further.

She would find his killer.

After a while, she turned away from the window. "I'd better go. Mom will be calling the loft to see if I'm back." She attempted a smile. "She's a little gun-shy about mountain driving these days."

"I'm sure she is." Wally rose from behind his desk. As they walked in silence toward the door, he wrapped a comforting arm around her shoulders. Out in the small parking lot, Jill kissed him on the cheek. "I'm sorry I gave you a hard time in there."

He made a dismissing gesture. "You did no such thing." He returned the kiss. "Don't be a stranger, now, you hear?"

"I won't."

He watched her walk toward her old green BMW, her stride quick and brisk, like her father's. As she backed the old sports car from its parking space, she touched the horn once and waved. He returned the wave, wishing he had the power to make her happy again. Then, with a sigh of resignation, and a silent promise to call her in a couple of days, he walked back inside.

Two

It was six o'clock by the time Jill returned to Greenwich Village where she had lived for the past thirteen years. After parking her car in her usual spot at the garage off Washington Square, she headed south toward MacDougal Street.

Once a mecca for street peddlers and drug addicts, Greenwich Village, or the West Village, as the locals called it, had undergone a gentrification of sorts over the last two decades. A new, more artistic crowd had moved in—writers, painters, jazz musicians and, of course, the inescapable aspiring actors without whom New York wouldn't be New York.

With the arrival of nighttime, the thick clouds that had threatened to spill open earlier had dissipated, and a cold wind blew in off the Hudson, sending pedestrians scurrying home.

On an impulse, Jill stopped at Eddie's Market, the small grocery store on Bleeker Street, to pick up what she needed to make an omelette. She even treated herself to a slice of Eddie's homemade pumpkin pie and a container of Cool Whip. She always functioned better when her sweet tooth was satisfied.

A few minutes later, she opened the door to her loft, and was immediately enveloped by its comforting warmth and familiar smells. Although the one-bedroom apartment was only a fraction of the size of the Upper East Side town house where she had been raised, these modest quarters had become her sanctuary, the only place where she felt truly at home.

She had fallen in love with the loft the moment she had laid eyes on it in the summer of 1984. She hadn't been looking for just a home at the time, but a love nest, a place for her and Dan to start their married life together.

Two days later, they had signed the lease.

There had been many changes since then. The marriage had ended in divorce a year later, and the apartment, which she had purchased when the owner had converted the building to condominiums, had undergone a complete makeover. The cheap furnishings she and Dan had bought at a New Jersey flea market had been replaced by heavy oak tables, plump sofas in bold floral chintzes and Turkish throw rugs. The tiny kitchen now boasted new, state-of-the-art appliances, and the bathroom, unusually large for this part of town, had been redone in marble tiles of varying blue hues.

Jill's decision not to move back home after her divorce had baffled her father. He couldn't understand why she would choose the inconvenience, not to mention the hazards, of a downtown location, when she could live with them in the lap of luxury.

She hadn't tried to explain it to him. How could she when she couldn't even explain it to herself? When she wasn't sure if her decision stemmed from a need for independence or from her reluctance to let go of the last thread that linked her to Dan Santini?

As Jill put away the groceries, her glance fell on the sympathy card on the kitchen counter. Her ex-husband's condolences had arrived three days after her father's memorial service. The message, written in the familiar bold handwriting, was brief and to the point, another of Dan's trademarks.

Dear Jill:
    I was truly sorry to hear about your father. I found out too late or I would have come to the memorial service.
    Please extend my sincere sympathy to your mother and the rest of your family.

                                                    Dan.

Dan. Once, the mere sound of that name had been enough to send shivers of pleasure down her spine. Nowadays, the only emotion she could conjure, even after all this time, was a deep resentment. And why shouldn't she be resentful? He was the one responsible for the breakup of their marriage. If he hadn't been so damned proud, so damned determined to do it all with no help whatsoever from anyone, they'd still be together right now.

From the built-in wine rack above the sink, she took a bottle of Châteauneuf du Pape and started to uncork it with quick, angry movements. If she still harbored such ill feelings for her former husband, why was she thinking so much about him these days? Why were memories popping up at her from every nook and cranny of this apartment?

A soft knock at the front door saved her from answering a question she didn't want to consider in the first place. "Who is it?" she called over her shoulder.

"Ashley."

The voice made her smile. Suddenly in a better mood, Jill went to answer the door. "Hi there."

Ashley Hughes, whom she had known since her sophomore year at Columbia, owned the vintage clothing boutique across the street and lived one floor below. She was a petite, effervescent young woman with long, frizzy brown hair and intelligent green eyes. Her little granny glasses made her look older than her thirty-three years and more vulnerable than she really was. Ashley and her husband, Drew, had been living in the building for over a year when Jill and Dan moved in. In fact, Ashley was the one who had told them about the vacancy. Their marriage had lasted longer than Jill and Dan's, but in the end it hadn't survived Drew's incorrigible womanizing.

"I heard you come in," Ashley said, holding up a steaming casserole rich with the aroma of garlic and fresh tomato sauce. "And thought you might be in the mood for some down-to-earth food."

"Ashley Hughes, you are a godsend." The yet-to-be omelette forgotten, Jill bent toward her friend's offering and closed her eyes. "Mmm. Chicken cacciatore?"

Ashley walked past her. "Close but no cigar." She set the casserole on the counter. "It's spinach lasagna. And there's enough for two, so if you don't mind I'll join you. I worked all day without a single break and I'm starved."

"The Summerfield wedding again?" Jill took two

stemmed glasses from a cupboard and set them on the counter.

"How did you guess?"

"I've seen that murderous look in your eyes before, usually after one of Lucinda Summerfield's visits."

Ashley blew a breath that made her curly bangs flutter.

"That woman is, without a doubt, the mother of the bride from hell."

"What has she done now?"

"She has decided, six days before the wedding, mind you, that her daughter's wedding dress doesn't have enough of a 1920s look. Never mind that the gown was made in 1923 and is absolutely perfect as is, she wants me to add a three-foot train to it. Can you believe it? She's going to ruin the look. Not to mention how long it will take for me to match the antique material."

"What does her daughter say? It's her wedding, after all."

Ashley opened a drawer, took out two yellow place mats and arranged them on the drop-leaf table against the wall. "The poor girl is about to self-destruct. Hopefully, she'll wait until *after* the wedding to do it." She accepted the glass Jill was offering and took a sip. "How about your day? I hope it was more rewarding than mine."

"Not really." Jill's expression was thoughtful as she gazed into her glass. "I went to see Wally."

"And?"

"He's closing the case, Ash, and I can't say I blame him."

"He didn't find anything?"

"Nothing to indicate that foul play was involved."

"Maybe that's because there *was* no foul play," Ashley said gently. "Maybe your father's death was an accident, after all."

Jill didn't reply. So many people had told her that, it was a wonder she wasn't beginning to believe it herself. "I don't know, Ash. Too many things don't add up—my father's nervous behavior, his drinking on the night he died, when he knew he had to drive back to New York." She took a sip of her wine. "And that damned gun permit," she added. "If it wasn't for that, I might be more receptive to the accident theory. Now I can't. My father was worried about something, or someone, enough that he thought it necessary to protect himself."

"He may have just been concerned about the rising crime rate. He was often working late, wasn't he?"

"Yes, he was, but I've never heard my father express fear or even one word of concern for his personal safety."

Ashley's gaze drifted to the kitchen counter where Dan's sympathy card still stood. Biting on her lower lip, she looked back at Jill. "If you feel so strongly about those suspicions of yours, why don't you call in the cavalry?"

Jill gave her a quizzical look. "Cavalry?"

"You know, someone experienced in that sort of thing, someone with an expert's knowledge of the criminal mind." Ashley took a sip of wine, glancing at Jill over the rim of her glass. "Someone like Dan."

Instant heat suffused Jill's cheeks. Words blurted out of her mouth so fast, she almost choked on them.

"Have you lost your mind? Why would I want to go to him?"

"Because he was the best homicide detective the NYPD ever had. And because at the time of your divorce, he told you if you ever needed him for anything, all you had to do was call."

"And I told him no, thanks."

Ashley chuckled. "That's not quite the way you put it." She narrowed her eyes in concentration. "I believe your exact words were 'When pigs fly.'"

Jill fought a smile. Had she really said that? Had she really been that immature? "Yes, well...I was having a tough day, but my feelings haven't changed. I would *never* ask Dan Santini for help. Besides, he's a college professor now. He's probably turned into a stuffy, boring nerd who wouldn't remember the first thing about investigating a real murder."

Ashley pursed her lips. "Hmm. Somehow I'm having a hard time imagining Dan as a stuffy, boring nerd."

"Well, I'm not." Mildly irritated that their conversation had suddenly centered on Dan, Jill shook off this strange mood she was in and forced all thoughts of her ex-husband out of her mind. "Now, can we stop talking about Dan and concentrate on food." She put her glass down, picked up Ashley's casserole from the kitchen counter and took it to the table. "All of a sudden, I'm famished."

Jill's taxi pulled close to the curb and stopped in front of the Vangram glass and steel tower at Fifty-ninth and Fifth where Bennett & Associates occupied the top four floors.

Simon Bennett, sometimes referred to as the high priest of modernism, had designed the skyscraper nearly three decades ago, creating a mild furor among conservative New Yorkers for his then-ultramodern design. Two months after the building's ground-breaking ceremony, a British bank had commissioned B&A to design a similar building to house their new U.S. headquarters in Los Angeles, catapulting Simon Bennett to the top of his profession almost overnight.

Glancing at her watch, Jill was relieved to see she was only a few minutes late. The message her uncle had left on her voice mail yesterday afternoon, requesting an early-morning meeting, had her worried. Since her father's death, B&A had already lost two important clients, both claiming that the death of the firm's leader put their projects in jeopardy. Neither Jill nor Cyrus had been able to convince them that B&A's talented team of architects, all of whom had been trained by Simon, were perfectly equipped to handle their project—any project. If this momentum continued, the future of B&A would be in serious trouble.

Crossing the wide atrium lobby, she hurried toward the bank of elevators in the back and rode up. In the fiftieth-floor lobby, a pretty receptionist sat behind a large console desk. She smiled when she saw Jill.

"Good morning, Miss Bennett."

"Good morning, Lucy." Jill walked briskly along the long green marble-floored gallery, where models of buildings B&A had designed over the years were prominently displayed, and headed for her uncle's office.

Cecilia, who had been her father's secretary for almost twenty years, was at her desk, stapling memos.

"Good morning, Cecilia. My uncle in?"

Cecilia Ramson lowered her stapler and looked up. Plump, discreet and efficient, she had been deeply affected by Simon's death and had gladly accepted Cyrus's request to stay on as his secretary.

At Jill's question, Cecilia nodded toward the closed door marked President. "He's been waiting for you, Jill. You can go right in."

Jill found her uncle buried in paperwork, his handsome face set into a perpetual frown as he tried to cut through a mountain of correspondence.

Although Jill had inherited the majority of her father's shares in the business, she and her mother had agreed that Cyrus was better equipped to be president of B&A than anyone else on the board of directors. Cyrus's subsequent decision that Jill step into the vacated vice-president position had met with the board's approval but had brought a new chill to the already strained relationship between Jill and Cyrus's stepdaughter, her cousin Olivia.

Aware that her uncle hadn't heard her come in, Jill closed the door behind her and stood looking at him. He was a big bear of a man, with graying red hair, the famous Bennett blue eyes and a broad, solid chest. She had never realized until recently how much he looked like her father. Sitting there, with his glasses perched halfway down his nose and that furrowed expression on his face, the resemblance was so striking that it brought a lump to her throat.

Suddenly, he looked up and grinned. "Hi, kiddo."

"How do you do that?" Lowering her slender body into a chair opposite his desk, she set her big suede bag on the floor. "How do you always know when someone is there?"

Removing his glasses and tossing them aside, Cyrus leaned back in his swivel chair. "Not just anyone. You. I'm not sure why that is. Must be something to do with mental telepathy."

There was some truth to that. She and Cyrus had always been close. Soul mates, he'd kidded her once. Next to her parents, he was her favorite person in the entire world. He was kind, thoughtful, intelligent and patient to a fault. And more important, he had always been there for her, professionally and personally.

It was he, rather than her father, who had attended all her dance recitals when she was a little girl, who had taken her to the zoo on Sundays and who had coached her first shaky seconds on a two-wheeler. Her father, busy with the launching of a company that was growing faster than anyone had expected, always seemed to be away or tied up in some important meeting during those early years. Jill realized how much she had come to rely on her uncle—and how much she needed him now.

"So, how did your visit with Wally go yesterday?"

"He hasn't changed his mind, Uncle Cy," she said, using the nickname she had given him when she was little. "He still believes Daddy's death was accidental."

"And you still don't."

Aware that he agreed with Wally on that point, she met his gaze without flinching. "I'm having a hard time with that theory, Uncle Cy."

Cyrus leaned forward, arms resting on his desk. "Jill, listen to me. You're a beautiful young woman.

You have your whole life in front of you. The last thing your father would want is for you to spend it chasing an imaginary killer.''

"I don't intend to do that, nor do I plan on neglecting my work here at B&A if that's what's worrying you."

"What's worrying me, kiddo, is *you*. You and this…this crusade you've taken on."

"There's no need to worry, I promise." She gave him a big smile. "Now, what did you want to see me about?"

Cyrus, never one to back away from an argument, started to say something, then stopped as though he knew he couldn't possibly win this fight. After a moment, he sighed. "I'm afraid I have bad news. The Maitland Group has decided to give the Church Hill Tower project to another firm."

Jill let out a groan. Church Hill Tower was a key, multimillion-dollar design of a sixty-four-story luxury-apartment complex in the heart of Richmond's historic Church Hill District. It was also Jill's first skyscraper outside New York City and a chance to establish herself as a major designer. To have the project taken from her now would be a crushing blow to her career.

"When did you find out?" she asked.

"Yesterday afternoon. Ben Maitland is afraid that, without your father, the creativity of the project will be compromised."

"But Church Hill Tower is *my* project. It's been my project from the beginning."

"I know, but Simon was there to supervise, and to advise, and that's what Ben and his associates fear will be missing. They have nothing against you, Jill. They

love your work. It's just that Simon was the reason
they gave us the commission in the first place and now
that he's gone..."

Jill slapped her palm against the armrest. "Dammit,
Uncle Cy, I'm not going to give up without a fight. I
spent six weeks of hard work on those preliminary
designs, and Ben Maitland and his five cronies are
going to look at them whether they want to or not. If
they still want to fire us after that, fine, but they're
going to do it in person, not through some crummy
phone call."

Looking more pleased than surprised by this sudden
heated outburst, Cyrus smiled. "You won't call them
cronies to their faces, will you?"

Despite Jill's bad mood, a smile found its way to
the corner of her mouth. "No."

"Good. How close are you to having the sketches
finished?"

"I'll have them done by Monday. It won't be easy,
but I can do it."

Cyrus gave a short, satisfied nod. "Then get to it.
And let me know if I can help, okay?"

"Thanks, Uncle Cy." Scooping up her purse, she
stood. At the door, she turned around. "By the way,
is Olivia in yet? I need to discuss something with
her."

"I saw her in the studio a few minutes ago. I believe
she came in early to help Griffin and his team prepare
for that *Architecture Magazine* competition next
month. She might still be there."

"Thanks." Jill left her uncle's office and went in
search of her cousin.

Three

A̲s usual at the noon hour, Body Perfect, one of Manhattan's most exclusive health clubs, was packed with harried executives anxious to sweat out their stress, well-toned models determined to stay that way and wealthy matrons hoping to stop the ravages of time.

Though Olivia Bennett didn't have a superfluous ounce of fat on her entire body, she came here every day for a punishing hour of aerobics, weight training and, time permitting, a dozen vigorous laps in the club's pool. At thirty-seven, and still single, one couldn't be too careful.

Her glossy black hair held back by a headband and her spectacular figure clad in purple spandex, she increased the speed on the treadmill and jogged more furiously. There was nothing like a good, sweaty workout to get the rage out of one's system. And after what Jill had pulled earlier this morning, rage was oozing from every pore.

Olivia hadn't always felt so vindictive toward her cousin. There had been a time when the two had been close friends, even best friends. But after Jill graduated from college, everything had changed. Olivia had been working in B&A's public relations department for a couple of years when Jill, a master's degree in architecture in her hand and stars in her eyes, had taken what she believed was her rightful place by her father's side.

From that moment on, the friendship had quickly deteriorated. Not even Olivia's promotion as director of PR years later helped bring down the wall that separated the two women. Jill's recent promotion to vice president had been the final blow, taking Olivia's hatred for her cousin to a new high.

"Slow down, Olivia, will you? I'm perspiring just watching you." On the next treadmill, her mother walked at a more moderate pace. At fifty-eight, Stephanie Bennett was an attractive woman with ash-blond hair, a pale, flawless complexion and a figure younger women at Body Perfect often admired.

Olivia showed no sign of slowing down. "If I do, I'll burst."

"What's wrong now?"

"Her Royal Highness, Queen Jill, is already flexing her muscles as the company's new vice president," Olivia said, breathing heavily. "She's written a memo stipulating that from now on all expenses over two hundred dollars be approved by her. She delivered it to me personally, along with a lecture about my high spending habits." She gave her moist forehead a quick swipe with the back of her hand. "How in hell am I supposed to run a decent PR department if I have to beg for every penny?"

"The company is going through a difficult period, Olivia."

"And whose fault is that?" Olivia's tone was plainly defiant. "If the board had listened to me, we'd be swimming in money right now."

"Oh, Olivia, selling Bennett & Associates to a big conglomerate is hardly a solution."

Olivia's arms pumped harder, as if the self-induced punishment helped release her rage. "On the contrary. It would be the perfect solution. The firm of Kasper & Willard has access to huge international projects we could never acquire on our own. Just think of the doors such a partnership would open—Europe, Asia, Australia—markets we might never be able to tap."

"Have you told that to Cyrus?"

Olivia made a derisive sound. "Of course I have. But he keeps siding with Jill. He always does."

"That's not true."

Olivia's dark eyes flashed as she glanced at her mother. "How can you say that? You know there's always been something special between those two. The way he talks about her, you'd think she was the only female in the company with brains. And when she makes a mistake, he's always there to bail her out. But let *me* do something wrong, and he reads me the riot act."

"That's because he loves you. He wants you to do well."

"Bull." Rivulets of perspiration ran down Olivia's face but she kept up the grueling pace. "He doesn't love me. He never did. He *tolerates* me because I'm his stepdaughter."

"Oh, Olivia, that's not true. You know how good Cyrus was to you after your father died. And he was never happier than the day he was finally able to adopt you and give you his name."

"That's because he and my real father were friends and he had promised him to look after us."

"No. It was much more than a promise made to a dying man. Cyrus truly loved you. He still does."

"But he loves Jill more." She spat out the words.

"Olivia, don't talk like that. Cyrus loves Jill because she's his niece and they have a long history together. Now that Simon is dead, he feels he has to protect her and help her through her grief. But he doesn't love her more than you. You have to get those silly thoughts out of your head. They're destroying you."

"Then why did he make her vice president instead of me?"

"Because those were Simon's wishes."

Across the room, an Arnold Schwarzenegger look-alike with muscles bulging struck a pose in front of the weight machine and darted a quick glance in Olivia's direction. She ignored him. Even though it had been weeks since her last romantic fling, she had never been less in the mood for a pickup.

"I deserved that position more than Jill did," Olivia continued, her breathing sounding more labored. "I'm the one with the seniority, and the experience. I'm the one who started from the ground up, delivered the mail, ran errands and sharpened pencils while I learned the business. Did Jill do the same? Oh, no." She let out a snicker. "Not the boss's daughter. In her first year at B&A she went right to the top, as her father's assistant. Was that fair, Mother? Was it?"

With the look of one accustomed to conceding defeat, Stephanie shook her head. "No, honey, it wasn't fair," she admitted. "But that's the way Simon wanted it."

Olivia's hand reached for the handlebar and

clenched it. "Nepotism," she said. "That's what it is."

"Maybe at first, but Simon wouldn't have kept her as his assistant if she hadn't lived up to his expectations. Jill is a damn good architect, Olivia. And a shrewd businesswoman, to boot. Even you have to admit that."

Breathing hard, though not totally from exertion, Olivia jabbed a button on the treadmill and cut the speed from five miles an hour to two. "I'm damn good at what I do, too," she muttered more to herself than to her mother. "But I never hear anyone singing my praises."

It was ten o'clock when Jill arrived at her mother's town house, a luxurious turn-of-the-century building on East Ninety-second Street. She had intended to have dinner with Amanda, but a last-minute conference call with an important West Coast client had kept her and Cyrus at the office well past the dinner hour.

Now, as Jill stood in the foyer, her gaze swept over the airy, sunken living room that had been the center of her family life for so many years. With its plush white sofas, pastel Aubusson carpets and collection of Chinese porcelain, the room was more a reflection of Amanda's expensive traditional tastes than Simon's, yet there was nothing pretentious about the decor. Like the rest of the house, the room conveyed a sense of space, light and total comfort.

"Ms. Bennett, I didn't hear you come in."

Jill turned to see Henry, her mother's butler, standing under the archway that opened onto the dining room. A small, slender man in his early sixties, he had worked for the Bennett family for twenty-eight years and was more like a relative than a servant.

As always, he was impeccably dressed in black pants, a starched white shirt and a striped black and gray vest.

"Hello, Henry." Jill jiggled her keys. "I let myself in."

He seemed pleased. "Would you like some dinner? It will only take a moment to reheat." He took her coat. "Chicken potpie. Homemade," he added as if Jill would find the thought too irresistible to turn down.

Jill smiled. Henry's mission in life, besides making her parents happy, had always been to keep her well fed. "I had something at the office, Henry, but thank you." She dropped the keys in her purse. "Did my mother go to bed?"

"A little while ago." He turned toward the wide curving staircase. "She might still be up—"

"That's okay. I don't want to disturb her. Actually, I stopped by to do some reading in my father's study. I shouldn't be more than an hour or so."

"Can I at least bring you something to drink? Tea? Coffee?"

"Tea will be fine."

He vanished as quietly as he had appeared, leaving her alone. Her mind already on the task ahead, Jill strode across the living room toward her father's study at the end of the hall. She wished she had a better idea of what she was looking for, but this was as good a place as any to start.

The room was just as her father had left it—orderly and smelling faintly of old books and expensive cigars. Simon's private sanctum, as Amanda called it, was everything he'd wanted it to be. Slickly lacquered walls in vivid red reflected deep black leather chairs and a floor-to-ceiling teak bookcase filled with dozens of books on modern architecture. Above the sofa stretched works of art by contemporary artists her father had admired—Dali, Warhol, Chamberlin. How well the room had suited her father, Jill thought.

She went through his desk quickly and found the usual office supplies—pens and pencils, a magnifying glass, several sheets of Bennett & Associates letterhead and an address book with the names of people she had known for years. At first glance, none had a motive to kill Simon, but it wouldn't hurt to make sure, though it wasn't clear how she would do that, either.

Equally disappointing were the two sets of drawers at the bottom of the bookcase, which were filled with art books and several works of literature. No one could have accused her father of not being well read.

In frustration, Jill slammed the last drawer shut, stood up from her crouched position and looked helplessly around the room. Her gaze stopped on a grouping of framed photographs on the opposite wall. Some of them were work-related—Simon standing in front of the now-famous Seigler Building in Houston, Simon smiling proudly at a ribbon-cutting ceremony, Simon shaking hands with then-President Reagan.

Other photographs were more personal and revealed bits and pieces of Simon's home life. Jill's favorite was the picture her mother had taken of Jill and her father dancing together at her sweet-sixteen party.

Around her neck was the gold chain and diamond teardrop he had given her earlier that day.

Fighting the tears, Jill studied the photograph. Not as powerfully built as Cyrus, Simon Bennett had nonetheless been an arresting man with bright red hair and lean, handsome features. His slight paunch was a testimony to his fondness for sweets, particularly Henry's incomparable Black Forest torte.

She was suddenly filled with an overwhelming sense of having let him down. "Oh, Daddy," she murmured, her eyes misting in spite of her efforts not to cry. "What happened up there? And how am I ever going to find out?"

A light knock at the door made her turn around. Henry walked in, carrying a tray with a steaming cup of her favorite Earl Grey tea and a small plate of almond cookies. "I thought these might tempt you." He nodded toward the delicate wafers. "I remember how they always made you smile when you were little."

"They still do, Henry." Jill watched as he lowered the laden tray onto a teak coffee table. "And how nice of you to remember."

"How could I forget? In those days you ate them faster than I could bake them." His face growing serious, he reached inside his breast pocket and pulled out a thick business-size envelope. "After the memorial service last week, your mother asked me to give Mr. Bennett's clothes to Goodwill, so prior to doing that, I sent everything to the cleaners and they sent this back." He looked at the envelope before handing it to Jill. "I was afraid it would upset your mother so I held on to it until I could give it to you."

"What is it?"

"A few personal items Mr. Wang found in one of your father's suits." His expression turned apologetic. "I'm sorry, Ms. Bennett. I must have forgotten to check the pockets..." Looking stricken, he let the words trail off.

"That's all right, Henry," Jill said gently. "None of us were functioning very well those first few days after my father's death." She opened the envelope and went through the items quickly. There was a monogrammed handkerchief, a tortoiseshell comb and a half roll of Certs.

"What's this?" Jill studied what looked like the passenger receipt for an airline ticket.

"I imagine that's Mr. Bennett's ticket to Miami. As I recall, he wore that suit the day he flew there."

Jill glanced at the receipt and frowned. "This ticket isn't for Miami." She looked up. "It's for Washington, D.C."

"It couldn't be." Henry took the ticket, looking confused. "I don't understand. October 3 and 4 are the dates Mr. Bennett went to Miami. I'm sure of it. I took him to the airport myself."

"Maybe he changed his plans at the last minute." But why? Jill thought. As one of three architects in the country vying for the design bid on the new Miami aquarium, her father had been anxious to attend that meeting. Jill remembered his irritation when the commission was later given to a rival firm.

"Maybe your mother would know," Henry suggested. "Or Cecilia at the office."

"I'll check with them in the morning."

There had to be a simple explanation for this, Jill thought after Henry left. Her father flew to every part of the United States several times a year. Why was she getting herself all worked up over an unexplained trip? But after a while, her curiosity got the best of her. Gambling that Cecilia, who rarely went to bed before eleven, was still up, Jill picked up a cordless phone on the coffee table and dialed the secretary's number.

The phone rang twice.

"Hello?"

"Cecilia, it's Jill."

The voice at the other end was wide-awake, and gently scolding. "Jill, are you working late again?"

"No, I'm at my mother's house." Aware that Cecilia was a confidential secretary in the true sense of the word, Jill hesitated, but only for an instant. She had questions that needed answers and Cecilia was the most reliable source she knew.

"Cecilia, do you remember that trip my father took on October 3 and 4?"

"Certainly." There was no hesitation in the secretary's voice, no indication that she was withholding anything. "He went to Miami to meet with Carl Jenner, who's heading up the committee for the new aquarium."

"Do you know if my father changed his plans at the last minute? I mean, could he have gone somewhere else instead?"

"Without telling me? I doubt that very much. You know what a stickler he was about leaving a complete itinerary." Cecilia paused. "Why all these questions, Jill? What's going on?"

"An airline stub was found in one of my father's suits," Jill said as she gazed at the receipt in her hand.

"It's in his name, for the right dates, but the destination is not Miami. It's Washington, D.C."

"That's strange. He never told me about a change of plans." Cecilia fell silent.

"Do you have any idea what he could have been doing in Washington? Who he went to see?"

"I don't have a clue. Washington wasn't one of his usual destinations. Maybe you should call Carl Jenner. He could tell you if your father went to Miami or not. I can give you his home number if you'd like."

"I have it, thank you." Jill hung up, then flipped through the address book she'd found in her father's desk, before dialing again.

On the first ring, a servant with a strong Spanish accent answered and put her through to Carl Jenner.

"Jill! How are you, my dear? I was terribly sorry to hear about your father. He'll be greatly missed."

"Thank you, Carl."

"You know, I never had a chance to tell you how disappointed I was that we won't be working together on the aquarium project. Even without your father at the helm, I feel certain Bennett & Associates would have done a terrific job."

Jill stared at a crystal paperweight on her father's desk. What an odd thing to say for a man who had turned down their bid.

"I was disappointed, too," Jill said politely, "but the reason I called is that there seems to be some sort of mix-up with our travel agency regarding a bill. Could you verify exactly when my father came to Miami? The meeting with you was on October 3, wasn't it?"

"Why, yes, it was." His voice sounded strange,

puzzled. "But your father canceled that meeting. He called the day before and told me an emergency had come up and he wouldn't be able to make it."

"I see," Jill said. But she didn't see. Not one bit.

Fortunately, Carl didn't seem to notice her confusion. "At the time your father called, I felt confident I could reschedule the meeting and told him so." Carl's sigh was filled with regret. "Unfortunately, the committee insisted on making a decision right away."

"I understand." She understood nothing. Carl's explanation was not at all the one her father had given her. "I guess the travel agency must have made a mistake, after all."

She hung up slowly and gently drummed her fingers on the desk. What Carl had just told her wasn't making any sense. She remembered her father's excitement when the committee chairman had called him in September to tell him B&A had been short-listed. He had even ordered a bottle of Dom Pérignon and called the board into his office to celebrate.

What in the world could have happened between that jubilant day and October 3?

And just what emergency had her father kept so well hidden?

Four

"Place your bets, please." The dealer's sharp gaze swept over the roulette table as he picked up the steel ball and prepared to throw it.

Dressed in a beaded dark blue silk suit that skimmed her perfect figure, Olivia Bennett chewed on her bottom lip while considering her next bet.

Her decision to drive to Atlantic City after work had been made as she rode down the crowded elevator of the Vangram Building, wondering how to spend the evening. Stressed out as she was, a short visit to her favorite casino had seemed like the right antidote for a rotten day.

So far, the evening had been a total bust. She had been gambling for nearly two hours and her hopes of recovering her losses were quickly fading. Clearly, this was not her night.

As the dealer repeated his warning, Olivia counted ten chips, each worth fifty dollars, stacked them in a pile and pushed them slowly across the table, stopping on number fifteen black.

She had been fifteen when she lost her virginity. That ought to count for something.

"No more bets." The dealer gave the wheel a snap

of the wrist and threw the metal ball in the opposite direction.

The marker stopped on three red. Olivia closed her eyes and bit off a curse. Her losses to the casino for the month now amounted to a little over five thousand dollars.

She knew she should call it a night and be glad she hadn't had to hock her car, as that poor woman next to her had done earlier. But in spite of her little pep talk, the table beckoned, coaxing her to stay and to place one more bet, the one that would turn her luck around.

Glancing to the side, she searched for the pit boss she knew was never very far away. When she spotted him, she gave a slight nod. Hands behind his back, he came up beside her. Tonight, his thin, pinched features looked more hawklike than ever.

"What can I do for you, Miss Bennett?"

She gave him her most beguiling smile and hoped he wouldn't notice how frantic she was to get back into the game. While the Golden Palace catered to heavy rollers, they insisted on prompt payment of all debts.

"I need another extension on my credit line, Charles." She tried to keep the tremor from her voice. "A thousand should do it."

The man's expression didn't change. "I'm afraid that's not possible, Miss Bennett. You're already well over your limit—"

"I'm also one of your best customers, Charles." Her tone sharpened. "Let's not forget that."

The pit boss, trained to handle hundreds of gamblers

every day, remained unfazed. "I'm sorry, Miss Bennett. I have my orders."

Olivia considered reminding him that her firm had designed the Golden Palace and that she was the one who had persuaded the editors of *Architecture Magazine* to put the hotel-casino on the front cover of their publication last year.

She did neither. She was already *persona non grata* in two other casinos. She couldn't afford to alienate a third.

Trying to be as inconspicuous as possible, she thanked Charles and climbed off her stool. As she turned to leave, she stopped in her tracks. Pete Mulligan stood less than three feet away from her, one shoulder braced against a Grecian column. He was watching her with an amused expression, his keen eyes missing nothing.

In his late forties, the owner of Mulligan & Son had taken over his father's construction business two years earlier but had yet to bid successfully on one of B&A's designs. Shortly before Simon's death, the two men had had strong words on that subject, with Mulligan accusing Simon of illegally manipulating the bids and Simon throwing the contractor out of his office.

Handsome in a rugged sort of way, the younger Mulligan had thick black hair, intense dark eyes and a cocky attitude that had irritated the hell out of Simon.

Mildly curious, she watched him detach himself from the column and walk toward her. "Miss Bennett. What a pleasant surprise."

A small warning bell rang in Olivia's head. If there

was one thing she didn't believe in, it was coincidences. "Good evening, Mr. Mulligan. Fancy meeting you here."

"Everyone needs to unwind." His glance slid casually toward the roulette table where the action had resumed without Olivia. "As a matter of fact, I was about to have one last drink before hitting the road," he continued. "Like to join me?"

"I don't think so." Not wanting to appear rude— she was, after all, in the public relations business— she tempered her rejection with a smile. "I have a long drive ahead of me."

"Oh, come on, a quick one. Club soda, of course, since you're driving." He leaned forward, his tone softer, almost caressing. "I promise you won't regret it."

Her curiosity piqued, Olivia frowned. "What does that mean?"

"You'll see." Taking her elbow, the contractor escorted her to an out-of-the-way table in the nearby lounge where he ordered two club sodas.

"I see you like to gamble," he said when they were settled. The thought seemed to please him.

Denying it would have been pointless. She was now certain that he had not only been watching her but had overheard her conversation with the pit boss, as well. "Occasionally."

"Expensive habit."

"My habits are nobody's business," she said sharply.

"True. I'm sorry." But he didn't look sorry. In fact, his amusement seemed to grow.

A waitress in a flouncy black skirt brought their drinks and quickly disappeared.

"To better luck at the tables," Mulligan said, lightly touching his glass to Olivia's.

Olivia sipped her club soda, wondering what he wanted with her. If he had orchestrated this "chance" meeting, as she suspected, what was his goal? What could he possibly want from her?

"So," she said, trying not to sound too eager. "Are you going to tell me what you meant when you said I wouldn't regret having a drink with you?"

His smile was mysterious. "I was referring to a little favor we might do for each other."

"Really." More and more intrigued, she waited.

"I couldn't help hearing your conversation with Charles a few minutes ago."

"You know Charles?"

"Quite well." He gave her that cocky smile again. "I, too, enjoy the tables every now and then." He leaned forward and lowered his voice as if he was about to confide in her. "How much are you in for?"

Olivia bristled. No one, not even her mother, knew about her regular trips to Atlantic City, but she sensed that Mulligan, whose connections some claimed extended to the Mafia, knew exactly how much she was in for. "None of your damn business." This time she didn't bother to smile. She didn't like people who snooped into her affairs.

The sharp reply didn't appear to faze him one bit. "Didn't you hear me? I want to help you."

"You also mentioned a favor."

"A small one." Mulligan hitched his chair closer until their knees touched. Then, with hardly a change in expression, he pulled out an envelope from his pocket and slid it across the table. "Here you are, Olivia, the end of all your problems. Ten grand. Five to get the people upstairs off your back and another five to have a little fun."

She didn't miss the subtle switch from "Miss Bennett" to "Olivia," as if they were already accomplices in some secret scheme.

Chewing on her bottom lip, she looked at the envelope but didn't touch it. There were a million reasons why she shouldn't take money from a slug like Mulligan—all of them valid. On the other hand, the manager of the Golden Palace had warned her that, if she didn't settle her account by week's end, he'd turn the matter over to a collection agency.

But she was too smart not to know that such generosity came at a high price. "What do you want from me in return?"

Mulligan leaned back. "I understand B&A was recently commissioned to design a six-story department store in Lower Manhattan."

"That's right."

"And your father is taking bids from various contractors."

Now she understood what he wanted, and the thought sent a cold shiver down her spine. But if there was one thing she had learned working in PR, it was the art of remaining cool. "So?"

"I want to know what the low bid is."

She shook her head. "I'm afraid I can't help you there."

"You haven't heard the rest of my terms yet."

Olivia studied Mulligan's dark, hooded eyes. What

he was asking was out of the question. It was much too risky. Almost sadly, she glanced at the bulging envelope. "The answer is still no."

"You're making a mistake, Olivia. You see, the ten thousand is just an incentive. If I get the job, which I expect to do with your help, I'll give you ten percent of my profits."

Olivia did some quick math. The hotel construction job was expected to bid for five million dollars, and would earn the contractor a fifth of that. Ten percent of a million was a hundred thousand dollars.

"It gets better," Mulligan continued. "With every job I get from B&A through you, I'll keep paying you the same fee." His glance wandered toward the casino floor. "Just think what you can do with that kind of money." His eyes gleamed as he waited for her answer. "What do you say, Olivia? You're interested?"

Olivia's heart began pumping hard. A hundred thousand dollars was indeed a lot of money. With a little restraint, she could make it last well into the spring.

Her throat went dry. What was she thinking? She couldn't do what he was asking. Rigging bids was illegal. What if she got caught?

On the table, the envelope seemed to grow thicker. Why would she get caught? All she had to do was get into her father's office when he wasn't there, look at the bids and call Mulligan. Who would know?

"Olivia?"

"I'll have to think about it." She wished she hadn't answered so quickly. It was never a good idea to let others see how desperate you were, even if they sensed it.

"Good enough." Mulligan drained his glass. "Meanwhile, you keep the money."

"I can't—"

"Sure you can. It ain't healthy owing money to a casino." He gave her a heavy wink. "You never know who they might be connected to."

Was that a casual remark? Or a veiled threat?

Trying to keep her hand steady, Olivia took the envelope and slid it into her purse.

"Call me in the morning." Mulligan gave her a knowing smile, as if he already knew what her answer would be.

Rising, she gave him a curt nod and walked out of the lounge, feeling the contractor's gaze cut into her back.

Outside the casino, Olivia, feeling richer than she had in months, handed the valet attendant a five-dollar bill and slid behind the wheel of her black Lexus.

Before driving away, she glanced at her reflection in the rearview mirror, and noticed her bloodshot eyes. She'd look like hell in the morning. She always did after a losing spell.

Well, at least now things were looking up. For one thing, her debt to the casino was paid in full. Next time she saw Charles, he would be bending over backward to please her. That was the name of the game in this town. Treated like royalty one day, like a pauper the next.

Her gambling habit had begun innocently enough. A year ago, on a boring Sunday afternoon, a friend had taken her to Atlantic City and taught her how to play roulette. In the first hour, Olivia had won six hundred dollars.

The win had been better than hundred-year-old brandy, better than sex. Money in hand, she had walked to one of the hotel's numerous gift shops and spent her winnings on a pair of Charles Jourdan shoes.

At first, Olivia had told herself that gambling was amusing, an entertaining pastime she could indulge in when nothing else seemed to excite her.

But after a couple of months, the occasional weekend escapades became more frequent, the stakes increasingly higher, the need to gamble stronger.

She wasn't sure when the habit had turned into a full-blown obsession. Suddenly, she had found herself in debt to everyone she knew—her mother, her friends, even an old lover or two. Last month, in desperation, she had refinanced her Sutton Place apartment and used the equity to repay some of her debts. Except for her five shares of B&A, which were useless to her at the moment since they couldn't be sold, and her salary, she was dead broke.

Worried the habit would destroy her financially, she had tried to get help, but the therapy class she had joined was a joke. A dozen misfits sat in a circle, listened to one another's sob stories and tried to figure out why they were so damn screwed up.

Olivia had lasted two sessions, and all she had learned for her three hundred dollars was that she had zero self-esteem, didn't trust people and had a deep-seated fear of intimacy.

Pressing on the accelerator, she merged smoothly onto the Garden State Parkway. *Fear of intimacy, my ass.* Was it her fault that she'd never found the right man? That every jerk she met turned out to be either married or unemployed or on coke?

She chuckled bitterly. Could she pick them or what? One loser after another. The story of her life—her private life, anyway.

As the glittering lights of Atlantic City disappeared behind her, she turned the radio to her favorite rhythm-and-blues station and let the soothing music wipe away the tension.

Sometimes the best way to deal with problems was to ignore them.

Jill returned from her mother's house with even more unanswered questions than she'd had earlier today. Too tired to work on the Church Hill designs, she sank into bed only to realize she was too keyed up to sleep. Hands clasped behind her head, she lay in the dark, trying to piece together a puzzle that was getting more complicated by the minute.

Reflecting on a conversation she'd had with her father back in October, his explanation of why B&A had lost the aquarium commission hadn't made much sense.

"Jenner wanted a local architect," he had told her. "Someone who could deal with unexpected problems immediately."

He had lied. And the big question was…why?

A nagging thought, one she had been rejecting all night, wormed its way into her mind again.

Another woman.

Jill shook her head, instantly denying the ugly accusation.

Her father was incapable of infidelity. He'd adored his wife, had adored her for thirty-six years.

And yet the thought remained, troublesome, persistent, like a headache that wouldn't go away.

Jill was still trying to sort through her tangled thoughts when dawn finally crept over the city, long hours later.

Five

"Mom, what a pleasant surprise!"

Smiling, Jill rose from behind her cluttered desk and walked across the spacious, well-appointed office to meet her mother. Amanda had made a valiant effort to pull herself together since her husband's death, but grief had taken its toll on her beautiful face. Her brown eyes, usually so bright and expressive, had dulled, and an unhealthy pallor clung to her otherwise flawless skin.

Yet there were some encouraging signs, Jill noted as her mother slipped out of her mink coat and draped it over a chair. Her short auburn hair had been recently styled and she had traded her mourning black for pale gray slacks and a white silk blouse.

"Henry said you wanted to see me." Amanda smiled, something she hadn't done in over a week. "So, here I am."

"Mom, you didn't have to do that. I was planning to stop by the house over my lunch hour."

"I know." Amanda laid her gloves on top of her coat. "But I thought it was time I started taking your advice and got out of the house a little. The fresh air will do me good, and so will getting out of Henry's way." She rested her gaze on Jill's desk, piled high with drawings. "Oh, dear, I've caught you at a bad time, haven't I?"

"Don't worry about it." Jill took her mother's hand. "I need a break anyway."

She led Amanda to an attractive grouping of blue upholstered chairs in front of the large plate-glass window. Below, the views of Central Park and the Woolman ice rink were unobstructed, and as pretty as a Currier and Ives scene.

"Would you like anything? Tea? My secretary should have something halfway decent tucked inside her drawer."

"Nothing at the moment." Folding her hands on her lap, Amanda gave her daughter a long, scrutinizing look. "Did you want to see me about anything in particular?"

Jill brushed an imaginary speck of lint from her impeccable brown skirt and hesitated. Her mother had made no secret that she didn't share Jill's suspicions regarding Simon's death.

"It's a ridiculous notion," Amanda had told her in no uncertain terms. "Give it up, Jill, and let your father rest in peace."

She wouldn't be happy to find out that her advice had been ignored.

Jill cleared her throat. "Do you remember that trip Daddy took on October 3?"

Irritation flickered in Amanda's eyes. "Jill, what is this? Are you playing detective again? I thought you were finished with that nonsense."

Jill decided to ignore the comment. "Do you remember that trip?" she repeated.

"Of course I remember it." Amanda's voice was laced with impatience. "Your father went to Miami."

"Is that what he told you?"

"It's where he *went*, Jill. You know that as well as I do."

Jill reached into her pocket, pulled out the airline receipt and handed it to her mother. "Take a look at this."

With an annoyed sigh, Amanda took the ticket and studied it for a moment. When she looked up, her face was a shade paler but her voice was steady. "Where did you find this?"

"Mr. Wang returned it. It was in one of the suits Henry brought to the cleaners after Daddy died."

Amanda's gaze went back to the ticket. Her hands tightened. "Washington, D.C.?"

"That's right. He never went to Miami."

"You don't know that."

"Yes, I do. I called Carl Jenner last night. He told me Daddy called him on the evening of October 2 and canceled their meeting. Daddy said an emergency had come up and he wouldn't be able to make it."

"That's ridiculous. What emergency?"

"I was hoping you could tell me."

"I'm afraid I can't." Amanda's hand went to her throat and began to massage it gently. "I'm sure it was just a business trip. He may even have mentioned it to me now that I think about it, but you know how forgetful I am about those things." There was an edge of tension in her voice.

Jill stiffened. Her mother was lying.

That realization left her speechless. Her parents had always been the foundation for everything Jill believed in, family, love, and above all, trust. That her mother was now lying to her, and in a sense betraying that trust, was both shocking and unsettling.

"Daddy never mentioned knowing anyone in Washington or the vicinity?" she asked at last. "An old friend perhaps? An army buddy?"

"No." Amanda shook her head firmly. "Never."

"Yet he went there. And he kept the trip a secret from all of us. Even Cecilia."

"You told Cecilia about this?"

"Mom, she was his private secretary, possibly the only person he could have told about his change in plans."

"Did he?"

"No. She was as bewildered as we are."

Amanda shot Jill a penetrating look. "Jill, where are you going with this?"

"I'm going after the truth. I want to know what happened to my father."

"We already know what happened." Amanda took out a lacy white handkerchief from her purse and pressed it delicately to one eye, then the other. "Nothing is going to change that."

Jill felt a quick wash of guilt. No matter what her mother was hiding, this kind of questioning so soon after Simon's death was cruel and unnecessary. Whatever mystery existed behind her father's Washington trip would have to be solved some other way. "I'm sorry, Mom. Please don't cry."

After one more quick dab at her eyes, Amanda tucked the handkerchief back into her purse. "Then promise me you'll—"

Jill's gaze abruptly shot toward the door.

"What's the matter?" Amanda asked, following her gaze.

"The door." Jill's shoulders tensed. She rose and walked quickly across the room. "Didn't you close it when you came in?"

"Of course I did."

But the door wasn't closed now. It was ajar.

A feeling of unease fluttered in Jill's stomach. Someone had been outside, listening to their conversation.

By the time Jill had reached the door and yanked it open, whoever had been standing outside was gone.

Cathie, Jill's secretary, had momentarily stepped away from her desk and hadn't seen anyone on her way back.

Now, as Jill sat in the cab that was taking her home after another long day spent working on the Church Hill project, she couldn't shake the doubts she'd had all day. Someone had been eavesdropping. But if so, who? A nosy secretary? A lost messenger? Or someone with a darker motive?

At the intersection of Fifth Avenue and Ninth Street, her cab stopped abruptly, the jolt interrupting her thoughts. The avenue was a sea of flashing red and blue lights as police and emergency vehicles blocked traffic in both directions. In the distance, the shrill whine of a siren was growing louder.

The driver turned in his seat. "Street clogged, miss," he said in a thick Oriental accent. "Sorry."

"That's all right." Jill was already pulling a handful of bills from her purse. "I'll get out right here."

"You sure?" He sounded concerned. "Village no

place to be late at night." He glanced at the cracked dashboard clock, which read midnight, and looked back at her, shaking his head.

"I'll be fine." She handed him his money, tipping him generously. "I hope you won't be stuck here too long."

Making her way through the maze of traffic, she lifted her coat collar around her face and started walking briskly away from the bright lights. An arctic wind had pushed the temperature down to the low teens, which accounted for the nearly deserted streets. As she approached Washington Square, she saw two young men in black leaning against a tree, smoking. It wasn't until she passed them and smelled the sweet, cloying odor that she realized they were smoking a joint.

Their boldness didn't shock her, or even surprise her.

While Greenwich Village was a quirky blend of artists and young professionals during the daylight hours, at night it turned into a haven for over-the-hill hookers, skinheads and other unsavory characters. Fortunately, tonight's frigid weather had kept most of them at bay.

Ten minutes later she reached MacDougal Street. A lively thoroughfare during the day, the narrow, empty street lay deep in shadows, the storefront windows dark and heavily barred. Two of the three streetlights on her block were still out, which was annoying but hardly surprising. With city funds shrinking more each year, it sometimes took weeks and dozens of irate complaints for the city to change a single lightbulb.

Feeling suddenly uneasy, Jill quickened her step while rummaging through her purse for her keys.

Maybe she should have listened to the cabbie's advice and waited.

She almost sighed with relief when her apartment building came into view.

She was about to unlock the street door when she sensed, rather than heard, a presence behind her.

Her skin prickled with fear. She spun around just in time to see a dark figure leap at her from behind a tall potted evergreen.

Instinct took hold and Jill broke into a run, dropping her purse in the process. She didn't stop to pick it up. If it was her money the man was after, he was welcome to it.

She raced back toward the square, passing the same darkened storefronts and doorways she had walked by a moment earlier. She tried to scream, but when she opened her mouth, no sound came out.

Flying feet pounded after her. Her breath heaving, Jill ran faster, her arms and legs pumping hard. The single light at the end of the street was like a beacon, spurring her on. Only a couple more blocks and...

She never had a chance to finish her thought. A hand seized a handful of her hair and yanked her back. With a gasp, she fell to the ground, and in a split second the man was straddling her.

To her horror, his gloved hands gripped her throat and began to squeeze.

In spite of her rising panic, Jill fought him hard, hooking her fingers around his and trying to loosen his grip while her legs kicked wildly. She could feel the blood rushing to her ears in a loud roar and knew she was losing the battle. She tried to see the man's face but it was smeared with something that resembled black polish.

She was going to die at the hands of a faceless killer.

"Hey, you!" a voice called out. "Let her go."

The warning caught the attacker by surprise. Though his face was still in shadows, Jill sensed a moment of hesitation on his part, as if he was debating between finishing the job he had started or running to safety.

His grip relaxed. Instantly, Jill splayed her hands against her assailant's chest and shoved with all the strength she could muster. Caught off guard, the man jerked back, then quickly scrambled to his feet and took off down MacDougal, away from the square.

"Are you all right?" The male voice sounded young. A second later, the man to whom she owed her life crouched beside her.

"Miss? You okay?"

Pulling herself to a sitting position, Jill took huge gulps of air. Her hand went to her throat. "I think so." She tried to sit up.

"Hey, take it easy," the stranger cautioned. Slipping an arm around her waist, he helped her up. "Did you get a look at him? Can you identify him?"

Jill shook her head. "Too dark. And his face was covered with something…a black paste."

A light in an upstairs window suddenly came on, casting a pale glow on the street below. Her breathing now under control, Jill took another look at her rescuer. And had another shock.

He was young, probably not yet out of his teens, and very thin. He wore black jeans, a black leather jacket and had a small gold ring in his right nostril. His hair, dyed an alarming shade of purple, rose straight above his head in dozens of heavily sprayed spikes. Five minutes ago, the mere sight of him would have been enough to send her running for cover. But now he was the most beautiful sight she had ever seen.

When she found her voice again, she extended her hand. "I'm Jill Bennett," she said.

His grip was remarkably firm. "Jerry Kranski."

"I owe you a big debt, Jerry. If you hadn't come to my rescue when you did..." She glanced down the street, but her attacker had long since disappeared. "I don't know what he would have done." She had started to say, "I'd be dead right now," but couldn't quite get the words out.

Her gratitude seemed to make the teenager ill at ease. "You sure you're okay? You should probably call the cops."

"I will when I get home." She had little hope the police would catch her assailant, but at the very least the incident might prompt the city to replace those burned-out lights.

"What were you doing out alone?"

Aware she was still shaking, Jill pushed her hair back with both hands. "I was on my way home from work."

"My mother's boss always gives her cab fare when she works late."

Jill almost laughed. The irony of the situation—a dangerous-looking teenager dispensing advice on street safety—didn't escape her. "I did take a cab, but we were held up in traffic, so I decided to walk the rest of the way."

Jerry looked around him. "So," he said hesitantly, "you want me to walk you home? In case this guy comes back?"

Jill wasn't in the habit of letting perfect strangers know where she lived. But in spite of his appearance, there was something trustworthy about the boy. And he *had* saved her life.

As if he had read her mind, Jerry gestured behind him, in the direction of Broadway. "I live a couple of blocks from here, over on Jones Street. My mother works at City Hall."

Jill smiled. She was definitely beginning to like this guy. "I'd like very much for you to walk me home, Jerry. As I said, I owe you a big debt and I intend to repay it."

"Hey, forget it. We're cool here. I just happened to be around, you know."

Her purse was still where she had dropped it, in the middle of the sidewalk. She started to bend down to pick it up but Jerry beat her to it.

For a moment, she wondered if he was going to take off with it. She felt foolish when he handed it to her.

"Here you go."

"Thank you." Together they walked back toward Jill's building. The streets seemed less threatening now that she was no longer alone, but the raw fear she had experienced a few moments earlier clung to her like a bad odor. She could still feel the man's powerful hands around her throat, hear her gasping breath.

She turned, worried he might still be lurking nearby, but didn't see anything.

Back in the small lobby of her apartment building, she flipped a switch on the wall. In full light, Jerry

Kranski wasn't quite as frightening as he had seemed in the dark street. Except for the blond fuzz on his right cheek, proving he was old enough to shave, his face was almost childlike, with baby blue eyes, a small mouth and a pimple on his chin. The look was a sharp contrast to the purple spikes and the nose ring, but maybe that mixture of tough guy and sweet kid was what Jill found so appealing about him.

"Well…" Under her stare he seemed to grow even more self-conscious. "If you're sure you're okay, I'd better go. My mom doesn't like it when I break curfew."

Jill pulled a business card from her purse. "Will your mother be home tomorrow morning?"

"I don't know. Why?" He looked suddenly suspicious.

"Because I'd like to stop by and tell her what a brave young man she has for a son. And because I want to do something for you," she added gently.

His chin went up a fraction of an inch. "I said we're cool with this. And I don't want any money."

"You saved my life, Jerry. That's not something I can ignore. Or ever forget." When he remained silent, Jill reached inside her purse again and pulled out a small address book. She handed it to him with a silver Cross pen. "Would you write down your address for me?"

She watched him as he wrote, noting his concentration as he formed each letter. "Thank you," she said when he was done. "I'll see you tomorrow then?"

He shrugged. "Yeah, I guess."

After locking the door behind him, Jill stepped into the elevator and punched the third-floor button. As the car began its slow ascent, she leaned against the mahogany panel and took a long breath. Her hands were shaking from her recent ordeal and she felt a pain in her tailbone where she had fallen.

But as images of the attack kept replaying in her head, what she began to realize was even more frightening than the attack itself.

What had happened to her was no accident.

Someone had just tried to kill her.

Six

J erry Kranski turned out to be exactly who he claimed to be, an eighteen-year-old high-school graduate with a mother who worked at City Hall and a nine-year-old sister named Ginny.

While Carol Kranski was very proud of her son's good deed, she had been adamant in her refusal to take money from Jill. Over coffee and thick slices of freshly baked raisin bread, the three of them had finally agreed that Jill's offer of a job at Bennett & Associates was a perfect compromise and couldn't have come at a better time. The electronics shop where Jerry had worked since graduation was closing down, leaving the teenager without a job.

"Don't worry about the hair," Carol told Jill as she walked her to the door an hour later. "Or the nose ring. As you can see, both come out during the day."

She glanced at her son, who was clearing away the coffee cups, and sighed. "He's a good boy, but sometimes it's hard for a single parent to compete with a teenager's peers. That's why I'm so happy about the job you just offered. It will give him an opportunity to make new friends."

Jill didn't know anything about parenting, but it wasn't so long since she had been a teenager herself—

a rather rebellious teenager. "I wasn't worried, Carol, and neither should you. Jerry seems to have some good, strong values and I know he'll do a fine job for us."

"Thanks for saying that. Oh, and by the way, I'll see what I can do about those burned-out streetlights. My boss works closely with the mayor and is always bragging he can get him to do anything he wants." She grinned. "I'll put him to the test first thing Monday morning."

"I'd appreciate that."

Jill hadn't been home more than five minutes when the doorbell rang.

"Jill, it's Ashley. Don't you *dare* hide from me."

Surprised at the simmering anger in her friend's voice, Jill hurried to open the door. Jill had never seen Ashley so upset. Her cheeks were flushed, her eyes bright with an expression that was a cross between fury and fear. A pincushion was strapped to her right wrist, suggesting she had left her shop in a hurry.

"Why would I hide from you?" Jill asked.

"Oh, don't play the innocent. I'm talking about you almost getting killed last night." She rested two tiny fists on her hips. "You weren't going to tell me, were you?"

Jill closed the door. "Frankly, no. I didn't want to worry you. You have enough on your mind with that crazy wedding. And if it makes you feel any better, I haven't told anyone else, except the police. Not even my mother."

"You didn't think I'd find out? In a neighborhood like this?"

"How *did* you find out?"

"I opened the shop early to finish the Summerfield bridal gown and two beat cops were already there, waiting for me. They'd heard I worked late every night and wanted to know if I had noticed anyone suspicious around the neighborhood yesterday evening. When I asked them what was going on, they told me what had happened to you and advised me to be on my guard."

Jill climbed onto the kitchen stool. "I had no idea they'd go around the neighborhood questioning people. When I filed the report last night, they said that without a description of the man, their chances of finding him were slim to none."

Ashley was too softhearted to stay mad for long. Her eyes filled with worry. Closing the distance between her and Jill with two quick steps, she gave her friend a fierce hug. "Oh, Jill, I got so scared when I heard. Did that beast really try to strangle you?"

"Yes, but I'm fine now." Jill patted her pink turtleneck. "I only have a few scratches and some bruises on my neck and a sore behind. Nothing more."

"The police said a neighbor saved you?"

"A teenager, a very brave teenager by the name of Jerry Kranski. If it hadn't been for him, you'd be planning my funeral right now." Her voice was shaky as she tried to laugh.

"And knowing you, you offered this kid a fortune."

"Couldn't. Neither he nor his mother would take any money, so Jerry is now an employee of B&A, or will be by Monday."

Ashley tried to smile and almost didn't make it. "Tell me what happened, Jill. Everything."

She listened quietly as Jill told her the details of her

attack and rescue. "Are you sure he was after you?" she asked when Jill was finished. "You don't think it could have been a random act of violence? Or a mugger?"

"That's what I thought at first. But..." Jill shook her head. "A mugger would have taken my purse. This man was waiting for me, Ash. I even had the feeling..."

"What?"

Jill held her friend's gaze. "That I knew him."

Ashley shivered. "Knew him from where?"

Jill rubbed the back of her neck. "I don't know."

"I just don't understand why somebody would want you dead. You're no threat to anyone." When Jill didn't answer, Ashley frowned. "Are you?"

"Maybe." Jill told her about her suspicions that someone had been listening outside her office door earlier.

"What were you and your mother talking about?"

Jill didn't answer right away. As much as she trusted Ashley, she couldn't bring herself to tell her that her father may have been having an affair. It was just too personal. Besides, she needed more answers. "I can't tell you, Ash. Not yet."

"That's fine." Ashley waved her hand. "Just tell me this, will you at least tell Wally?"

"I can't."

"Why not? You were almost *killed,* for God's sake. If you think that incident is tied to your father's death, Wally should know."

"But don't you see? I can't prove the attacker wasn't some kind of crazed mugger or a serial killer or some other maniac. Lord knows this city is full of them."

"Then all the more reason for you to quit what you're doing. Either that or hire a private detective."

"I can't do that, either. I can't let a stranger turn my family's lives upside down—especially my mother's. She's upset enough as it is without me adding to her anxieties by hiring a detective."

Jill could tell by the look on Ashley's face what she was going to say next. Before her friend had a chance to bring up Dan's name again, Jill glanced at her watch. "Look, I hate to be rude but I've got to get to work. Ben Maitland agreed to look at my sketches, but if I keep goofing off, they'll never be finished by Monday."

"I've got to get back to work myself." Ashley turned to leave. "Be careful."

Jill smiled. "Yes, ma'am."

His arm and leg movements perfectly synchronized, Dan Santini kept his speed even as he ran along the jogging path of Lake Shore Drive on Saturday morning.

Although the early-morning temperature registered a windchill factor of minus seven degrees, a handful of intrepid Chicagoans were already jogging up and down the famous drive, oblivious of the cold. A city for the hardy, Dan thought. That's why he liked it.

Short of a crippling blizzard, Dan never missed a day. The brisk exercise kept his mind clear and his body fit. Not to mention that it afforded him one of the best views in the entire city of Chicago. With Lake Michigan flowing silver on one side and the glinting city skyline on the other, the hundred-and-twenty-four-block drive was enough to entice even the most dedicated couch potato into some form of outdoor activity.

Running north, he passed the Planetarium, then Grant Park, home to several of the city's most famous museums. His long, effortless stride took him across the Chicago River and straight to Navy Pier Park, where he executed a broad circle and began to head back.

By the time he reached Mercy Hospital, where he had parked his car, he was sweating and feeling good. His watch read nine o'clock. Damn. He would have just enough time to drive home, shower and change before his meeting with the chief of police.

The meeting wouldn't be pleasant. Because of a rash of grisly murders in the South Side, Chief Brennan had asked Dan's assistance in catching the killer. The occasional requests from various police departments gave him an opportunity to put his experience with serial killers to good use and involve his students in a real case study.

Dan's phone was ringing when he walked into his Hyde Park studio apartment ten minutes later.

In two long strides he reached the end table and grabbed the receiver, sliding off his jacket as he did so. "Hello."

"Dan, it's Ashley Hughes. Jill's friend."

Instinctively, Dan tensed. "Is Jill okay?"

"Yes," Ashley said quickly. "I mean…she is *now*."

"Ashley, for God's sake, what's wrong with her?"

"Someone tried to kill her last night."

Dan felt as if he had been sucker punched. "Jesus Christ." He ran his fingers through his hair. "Where?"

"In front of her apartment building. It was late and some maniac came up from behind and tried to strangle her."

Dan's jaw clenched. "Are you sure she's all right?"

"Positive. A teenager who lives in the area came to her rescue."

Relief loosened the pressure in his chest. "Did they catch the bastard?"

"No. And it's not likely they will. It was too dark for her to identify the attacker." She paused. "She thinks it was intentional, Dan, that whoever attacked her wanted to kill her."

"Why would she think that?"

"She's been investigating her father's death. She doesn't believe that was an accident, either." Ashley's voice betrayed her anxiety. "And neither do I."

Under different circumstances, the thought of Jill playing amateur sleuth would have made him smile. She had always had a fertile and inquisitive mind and loved a good puzzle. That Nancy Drew side was one of the things he had loved most about her. But Ashley was right. This brutal attack had to be taken seriously.

"Did Jill ask you to call me?" he asked.

There was a low chuckle at the other end of the line. "Hardly. This was my idea, one I may soon live to regret." There was a brief, expectant pause. "You're the only one who can help her, Dan, the only one she'll listen to."

The remark made him laugh. "You have a short memory, Ashley. Jill was never very good in the listening department. Especially if *I* was the one dispensing the advice.''

''That was thirteen years ago. She's grown up a lot since then.''

Though he already knew the answer, he asked the question anyway. ''What exactly do you want me to do?''

Ashley let out a nervous laugh. ''Would finding the killer be too much to ask? Assuming Jill is right and Simon *was* murdered.

Dan was silent as he considered the request. Time wasn't a factor. With semester break just started, he had over a month of vacation coming. The trip to New York would even present a bonus—spending Christmas with his family in Brooklyn. Chief Brennan would be disappointed, but Dan could put him in touch with a former FBI agent who was an excellent profiler and lived only fifty miles out of Chicago.

The real question was more difficult. Did he want to get involved in Jill's life again? Stir up all those old memories? If the answer was no, then he was better off giving Ashley the name of a good private investigator in New York City. Of course, getting Jill to hire a P.I. when she was so determined to do the job herself might not be an easy task.

''Dan?'' Ashley's voice was heavy with worry.

''All right.'' Dan sighed. He was going to regret this, but what the hell. ''I'll take the first available flight.''

Seven

Dan arrived at the airport just in time to make the 11:02 flight to La Guardia Airport.

As he sipped a 7-Up the flight attendant had just poured him, he stared out the plane window, thinking about Jill, trying to anticipate her reaction and remembering his tempestuous marriage, in spite of the promise he'd made to himself not to.

She had a way of doing that to him, sneaking into his thoughts. Even now, after all these years.

He had met her in the spring of 1984. He was a police officer with the NYPD at the time and she was a sophomore at Columbia University. The odds of two such different people ever coming face-to-face, much less falling in love, were about a million to one. But on that balmy April night, the odds had been the last thing on his mind.

Dan was on his way home from work when he spotted the green BMW convertible parked on the side of the street in SoHo. The driver, a stunning redhead in a black evening gown, was standing beside the car, fists on her hips, glaring at a very flat rear tire.

When Dan stopped and offered to change it for her, she let out a sigh of relief and gratefully accepted his help. Hitching up her dress and crouching next to him, she told him that she had been at a party and hoped her father wouldn't realize it was almost 2:00 a.m.

"He doesn't seem to understand that I'm nineteen." She spoke as if she were thirty instead of nineteen. "And that I'm perfectly capable of taking care of myself."

As she talked, her scent enveloped him like a seductive cloud, toying with his senses and causing him to take longer with the tire than he needed to. While he slowly unscrewed each bolt, he had learned that she was studying to become an architect, like her father, and someday hoped to design skyscrapers all over the world.

She had great legs, he noticed. Even more seductive was the way she flipped those glorious red waves over one shoulder.

Ten minutes later Dan was finished and she was asking him for his phone number. "I want to thank you properly," she explained.

Dan wasn't quite prepared for what she meant by that. The following morning, after a personal thank-you from Simon Bennett himself, Jill stopped by the station and with the eyes of every officer in the squad room upon her, she walked up to Dan and invited him to lunch, her eyes gleaming with adoration.

It didn't take a genius to realize the kid had a major crush on him, a condition he had no intention of encouraging. Especially now that he knew about the vast disparity in their backgrounds.

Because she was young, vulnerable and very sweet, he had let her down gently, explaining she didn't owe him a thing. As a police officer, it was his duty to help citizens in distress. And, so there would be no misunderstanding, he had also explained that between his job and his part-time studies at NYU, he had no time whatsoever for a social life.

Far from being discouraged, Jill continued to call him every day. In fact, his excuses had become such a standard joke around the squad room that each morning, his colleagues hung around to hear the latest one.

Then, one day, tired of the teasing, Dan finally gave in and took Jill out to lunch—not to one of her fancy uptown eateries but to Mama Rosa, a tiny restaurant in Little Italy where the pasta primavera simply melted in your mouth.

As Jill devoured her meal and confessed her fondness for Italian food, Dan, captivated by her charm and absolute candor, fell under a spell he couldn't shake no matter how hard he tried.

Soon, the waiters, delighted by her enthusiasm for the food, brought her samples of other dishes. Even the cook came out to see who was the enchantress everyone was raving about.

Two months later, Dan and Jill were married, but not until Jill had agreed to one condition. They would live on his salary alone, without any help from her family—or her trust fund.

At first, they were blissfully happy. They loved their loft and Greenwich Village, which they explored together whenever their schedules would allow. And Jill, a child at heart, never tired of watching him perform some of the magic tricks he had learned from his uncle Guido.

But little by little, problems began to surface. Their most serious disagreement occurred when Dan gave up his courses at NYU and took a second job—tutoring college students—so he could pay for Jill's tuition.

"But that's silly," she argued. "My tuition has nothing to do with you. It's a commitment I made before I met you. Therefore, it's my responsibility and should come out of my trust fund." Hoping to end the argument, she added, "Besides, my money is your money now and being hardheaded about it isn't going to change a thing."

Dan's immense pride wouldn't allow him to accept Jill's rationalization. No man in his family had ever taken one single penny from a woman and neither would he.

He wasn't sure when the real trouble began. It was too subtle at first for either of them to detect it. But as the weeks and months passed, Jill became more and more restless. She complained that he was working too much and that she was beginning to feel more like a widow than a newlywed.

"It'll be different once I make detective," Dan kept telling her. "Be patient, Jill."

The arguments kept erupting, virtual shouting matches that almost always ended in bitter accusations and slammed doors.

One week before their first wedding anniversary, Dan asked Jill for a divorce.

Looking back at that year, Dan realized he hadn't had a clue what married life was all about. He had lacked patience and understanding and had been too focused on carrying the financial burden alone. In the process, he had overlooked one of the most fundamental requirements of marriage—to work as a team.

When he had finally realized his mistakes, it was too late.

As the years passed, he'd had to face another truth. He would never get over Jill. Not that he hadn't tried. He'd dated often. He had even come close to remarrying—just so he could prove to himself that he no longer gave a damn about his ex-wife. On the day he'd been about to propose, he had realized that marrying a woman he didn't love in order to forget the one he did love was a lousy foundation for a lasting relationship.

Twenty thousand feet below, the sprawling vastness of New York City and its five boroughs came into view, obliterating the memories. As the Fasten Your Seatbelt sign lit up and the Boeing 737 began its final descent into La Guardia Airport, Dan finished the last of his 7-Up and handed the empty glass to the flight attendant.

Maybe seeing Jill again was the answer to his problem. Maybe now he'd finally get her out of his system.

Three hours later, Dan parked his rented Land Rover on Brooklyn's busy Eighteenth Avenue in Bensonhurst, where he had grown up. Getting out of the car, he looked around, feeling the same nostalgia he always experienced each time he came back here. Home.

Bensonhurst was Brooklyn's answer to Manhattan's Little Italy. It was a neighborhood rich in traditions and, for Dan, filled with memories of a full, happy childhood. He passed the corner where he had played stickball with his two brothers after school, and the store where he had sipped thick strawberry shakes.

Later, in their teens, they had cruised up and down the street in Dan's first car, a 1968 Mustang he had buffed and coddled like a priceless jewel.

Brooklyn had changed over the years, but somehow this section of town had remained untouched. Not only was Santini's Deli still there, catering to the same old clientele, but so was the shoe-repair shop next door and the bridal boutique at the end of the block. Even the old movie theater, where the Santini brothers had spent every Saturday afternoon, was still standing.

Dan pushed the door to the deli and walked in. Behind the counter, Angelina Santini, a gray apron around her waist, had taken a braid of fresh mozzarella from the display case and was placing it on the scale.

At sixty-seven, Mario Santini's widow had stood the test of time and tragedy better than any woman Dan knew. Her face was plump and practically unlined, her eyes bright and sharp as she read the weight on the digital scale. She had buried one husband and one son and yet somehow had found the strength to survive both events. Her energy and good humor were legendary, and while she no longer made her famous sausages, she still rose at dawn each morning to make fresh mozzarella.

He watched her as she quickly folded the heavy white paper twice, secured it with tape and handed it to her customer.

"Here you are, Mrs. Remundo. One pound of the freshest cheese in town. You find fresher, I'll give it to you free."

Her customer laughed. "Not much chance of that, I'm sure."

Angelina smiled and handed the woman her change.

As she looked up, she saw Dan. Her mouth opened. "Danny!"

Stepping down from behind the counter, she ran to him as fast as her short legs would allow. "I can't believe it's you."

Laughing, Dan closed his arms around her and gave her a warm embrace. "Hello, Ma."

Her eyes were bright with tears as she held his face between her callused hands. "What are you *doing* here? When did you get in?"

"Just got off the plane, Ma."

Linking her arm through his, Angelina turned to her customer. "Mrs. Remundo," she said proudly, "I don't think you know my older son, Danny. He's the college professor."

Dan shook the offered hand.

"I just moved into the neighborhood," Mrs. Remundo explained. "Your mother talks about you all the time." She laughed. "She's as proud of you as she is of her cheese."

"Why didn't you let us know you were coming?" Angelina scolded when they were alone. "Your brother would have come to pick you up. And I could have prepared your room."

"I don't want you to fuss, Ma. I'll prepare my own room."

"Then you're staying for Christmas?" The excitement in her voice did his heart good. "This isn't one of your hurried visits?"

"I'll stay for Christmas. Even longer if you'll have me."

"If I'll have you?" Angelina gave him a playful push. "What kind of remark is that?" Her hazel eyes, so much like Dan's, clouded. "Did you get a chance to talk to Jill?"

"I tried but she wasn't home."

"You should have called Amanda's house. That's where she stayed for a few days."

"Then you talked to her?"

Angelina nodded. "That poor girl. She was trying to be strong, but I could tell it was all an act. I did the same thing myself when your father passed away, bless his soul." She gave Dan a searching glance. "When are you planning to go see her?"

Dan smiled. "Now what makes you think I'm going to do that?"

Angelina's eyes took on that old sparkle he knew so well. "Because, *filio mio*, I know you better than you know yourself. One look at you and I can tell you didn't come here just to spend Christmas with your family. You knew Jill was going through a difficult time and you wanted to see her."

It was too close to the truth, which didn't really surprise him. His mother had always had a keen sense of observation. "I give up, Ma, you're just too smart for me."

She tweaked his cheek the way she used to when he was a boy. "And don't you forget it." Then, because no one in his family could talk for very long without mentioning food, she added, "Are you hungry? Do you want something to eat? I just received a shipment of that Parma ham you like. I could make you a sandwich and some—"

"Ma." Dan gripped her arms and forced her to stand still. "It's two o'clock in the afternoon."

"So? People can't eat at two in the afternoon?"

"Only if they're hungry, which I'm not."

She made a disapproving click with her tongue. "You young people, the way you eat these days, it's a wonder you're not all skin and bones."

"Stop worrying about me, Ma. I take good care of myself." Through an open curtain, he caught a glimpse of the back room where his mother made her cheese and stored her supplies. His brother's apron with the caricature of a fat, jolly policeman on the front, hung on a hook. "Is Joe at the station?"

Angelina nodded. "He has the eight-to-four shift this week. Maria is out Christmas shopping and the boys are in school, counting the days until Christmas vacation. They're going to be so happy to see you, Danny."

"And I can't wait to see them."

Taking Dan by the arm, Angelina pushed him gently toward the door. "They won't be here for a while yet, so why don't you go see Jill and do what you have to do. By the time you get back, I'll have a nice homecoming dinner ready. Maybe I'll make those stuffed shells you like so much. And shrimp carbonara. Or would you prefer some bracciolo..."

Dan smiled. He was home.

Eight

Wearing an old sweatshirt and a pair of jeans, Jill thanked the messenger, took the envelope he handed her and closed the door.

The airline folder her travel agent had prepared for her came complete with a round-trip ticket to Richmond, Virginia, with a two-hour layover in Washington, D.C., on the way back, an itinerary, boarding passes and a half-dozen plastic luggage tags.

Now that the trip was actually booked, Jill was eager to start putting this damn puzzle together. And hopefully, catch a killer.

Instinctively, her hand went to her throat, still covered with a turtleneck. Physically, all that was left of last night's attack were some bruises, a few scratches on her neck, where her fingernails had dug trying to loosen the man's grip and an ugly red scrape on her tailbone where she had hit the pavement. There were other scars, but those were psychological and would heal, as well, though maybe not as rapidly.

She was still checking the tickets, making sure everything was in order when the doorbell rang. She walked back to the door, but did not open it immediately. "Who is it?"

"Dan."

A mild jolt went through her and she wasn't sure how long she stood there, rooted to the floor, aware of the flood of mixed emotions—bewilderment, anger, pain. When she finally opened the door, the shock of seeing Dan on her doorstep after all those years was so overwhelming that she could neither move nor speak.

"Hello, Red."

The familiar nickname brought a rush of memories she tried to ignore. As always, he exuded total self-confidence. Hands in his pockets, a light smile on his lips, he gave her a quick appraising glance. For an instant, only an instant, she couldn't draw a breath.

"What are you doing here?" she finally said. The sharpness of her tone annoyed her. No matter how much his presence rattled her, she must not let him see it.

"May I come in?"

Answer a question with a question. That, too, was a Dan Santini trademark.

Her first impulse was to slam the door in his face. That ought to answer his stupid question. Who did he think he was, barging into her life, unannounced, acting as though he had every right to be here?

But instead of closing the door, she opened it wider, watching him as he walked in. Physically, the last twelve years hadn't changed him much. The few lines around his hazel eyes were too fine to be called wrinkles and his jet-black hair was cut shorter, making him look youthful, yet more serious. That stubborn strand was still there, though, falling rakishly over his forehead, reminding her of the many times she had brushed it back.

Under the leather bomber jacket, his shoulders looked broad, his chest solid. He still didn't look like a cop, Jill thought. And he certainly didn't look like a college professor—none she knew, anyway. She, on the other hand, was a total disaster.

In a half-conscious gesture, she ran her fingers through her curls in a feeble attempt to tame them, then silently cursed herself for this show of vanity. Why should she give a damn how she looked?

"I'm sorry about your father, Jill." There was genuine sorrow in his voice. "I tried to call, but you weren't home."

She didn't want to discuss her father with him, partly because it was none of his business and partly because Dan had a way of drawing emotions out of her that always left her drained but somehow strangely at peace with herself.

That was not the way she wanted to feel right now. "You didn't answer my question," she said curtly. "What are you doing here?"

"I was in the neighborhood and thought I'd come up and say hi."

"Liar."

Dan held her challenging gaze and his intention not to be drawn into the depth of those wide-set blue eyes flew out the window. God, she was even more beautiful than he remembered. There was a new maturity to her face that hadn't been there before, an odd combination of strength and vulnerability. Only the hair hadn't changed. Though shorter, it was that same rich rusty color he had loved so much. Through the window, the last rays of the setting sun spilled over those glorious waves, making them look as if they were on fire.

She wasn't just beautiful anymore, he thought, trying to swallow past the knot in his throat. She was captivating.

So much for getting her out of his system.

Instinctively, his gaze traveled to her left hand. There was no wedding band on her ring finger, no engagement ring. He attributed the relief he felt to the fact that his task would be easier without a jealous husband or fiancé, underfoot. Deep down, he knew he was only kidding himself.

"Tell you what," he said, glad he had regained his voice. "I'll tell you why I'm really here if you invite me in for a cup of coffee."

She folded her arms over her chest. "You expect me to make you coffee?"

He held back a chuckle. Well, she hadn't changed *that* much. She still got riled over what she had always referred to as "the inequity of the sexes." "Would you rather I made it? I don't mind."

In a habit he remembered from long ago, she ran her tongue over her bottom lip. "That won't be necessary," she said pointedly. "I was about to make a pot, anyway."

He followed her across the small entryway and into the kitchen. The room bore only a vague resemblance to the one he remembered. Still small, it had a cheery yellow and white color theme, shiny new appliances and enough room for a drop-leaf table against the wall. His gaze, trained to see everything in one quick sweep, noted the airline ticket on the counter.

"Going somewhere?"

"Richmond, on Monday."

"For long?"

"Just for the day. One of our most important clients just fired us and I'm going there to try to make him reconsider."

"Why did he fire you?"

Jill shrugged. "Lack of faith. Now that Daddy's no longer at the helm, they're afraid we won't be able to do the job."

Jill busied herself with the coffeepot, filling the water tank, spooning ground French roast into the filter. "So," she said, keeping her back to him. "Why are you really here?"

"Ashley called."

Ashley. She should have known. "What did she tell you?"

"That someone tried to kill you."

"And that's why you came?" She was surprised, even touched, but refused to show it. He had always been such a gentleman, exasperatingly old-fashioned at times, but a gentleman nonetheless. "Sir Galahad to the rescue?"

He shrugged. "Something like that."

His voice was affecting her strangely. Now that he was here, so much of their life together was coming back—the day he had carried her over the threshold, the first time they had made love in their antique sleigh bed, the blizzard that had kept them housebound for three days, their first fight...

"You want to tell me what happened, Jill?"

Dan's gentle coaxing brought her back. "Why should I?"

"I'd like to help, that's all. Solving crimes is something I know a little about, remember? If your father was murdered—''

She spun around. "How do you know my father was murdered?"

"I don't. But I talked to Wally the day after your father's memorial service. He told me about your suspicions."

"You called Wally?"

"I was curious. My mother didn't have any of the details and I knew Wally would level with me."

"Did he tell you he didn't find anything to support those suspicions?"

"Yes."

She pushed a loose strand of hair behind one ear, another gesture Dan remembered well. Funny how all those little details kept popping out of his memory, as if they had been engraved there for years, without his knowledge.

"And you don't think I'm crazy?" she asked. "Or wasting my time?"

He focused his gaze on a point in the center of her back, a much safer target than that pink earlobe. "You've always had excellent instincts, Jill. If you think your father was killed, then it's probably worth looking into it—especially after what happened to you last night."

"I appreciate the good intentions, Dan, really, but this is something I need to handle on my own."

"So you can make yourself a target for this guy again?"

Jill opened a cabinet, took out two mugs and set them on the counter. "Next time I'll be ready for him."

"You can never be ready for a killer, Jill. If you learned anything as a cop's wife, surely you learned that."

She turned to look at him. "You're forgetting something, aren't you? I'm no longer your responsibility."

"Who said anything about responsibility? I just want to help. What's wrong with that?"

"Everything." She filled the mugs with strong aromatic coffee. "For one thing, I'd owe you."

That damn pride of hers again. It had always been every bit as deep as his own. "What if I told you I was doing it for Simon? I loved him, too, you know. When my father died, Simon was there for me. He saw me through a tough time and I've never forgotten it."

At the mention of Dan's father, Jill felt a quick stab of pain. Mario Santini had died suddenly, following a massive heart attack. The death, though quick for Mario, had been devastating for his family. Simon had given his son-in-law enough time to grieve, then in true fashion, had taken him on a week-long fly-fishing trip to the Catskills. Dan had come back a new man.

"What do you say, Jill?" He flashed her a disarming smile. "Will you let me help you? For old times' sake?"

She sipped her coffee, stalling. Maybe she had been too hasty in turning down his help. Determined though she was to find her father's killer, she didn't have a clue about how to conduct a criminal investigation. Or protect herself, for that matter. Dan, on the other hand, was an expert, with years of experience and remarkable detecting skills.

"If I do agree to let you help me," she said cautiously, "and I'm not saying I will—we work together. I'm not going to be shoved aside because some hot-shot detective has entered the picture."

"Fair enough. I'll probably need an assistant, any-way."

She laughed. "In your dreams, Santini. This is an equal partnership. I want to know everything you're doing, who you're talking to, every clue you—"

"And you'll do the same?"

"Of course." She had to force herself not to glance at the plane ticket on the counter. In all fairness, and if only to support the commitment she had just made, she should tell him about her planned trip to Wash-ington on Monday, but she wasn't ready to do that yet. And if her visit to the nation's capital didn't bring the result she hoped, she may not have to tell him at all.

She took a sip of coffee. "There's just one thing we need to settle before I agree to let you help me."

"What's that?"

"Your fee. I'd like to handle this arrangement in a businesslike manner."

She saw him stiffen. "There's no fee. I'm doing this because I want to."

"But that's not fair. Your time—"

"I'm not taking your money, Jill."

The sudden hard look in his eyes made her realize her money was still a touchy subject. Because she un-derstood that much better now than she had twelve years ago, she bowed her head. "All right. Thank you."

"You're welcome."

"I'd like to make something clear, though." She

refilled his cup. "There will be no strings attached to this deal."

"Of course not." He smiled, all trace of irritation gone.

"After it's all over, we both go our separate ways."

"I wouldn't have it any other way."

She looked at him for a long measuring second. "In that case...we have a deal. What do you need to know?"

"Start by telling me about last night." He was suddenly all business, almost crackling with energy, a condition Jill had always found contagious. "Is there anything about the man you remember? A fragrance you might have recognized? His build, the way he ran? Was he agile or clumsy? Did he breathe hard, like a man out of shape? Or did he seem athletic?"

"Yes," she said, astounded at the sudden clarity of certain details—details she hadn't thought about earlier. "I do remember certain things."

"Go ahead."

"He had to be in fairly good shape because he wasn't breathing nearly as hard as I was. When he ran away, he ran well, and fast."

"Was he a big man?"

"Not big in the sense of bulk, but he was strong. I don't remember a fragrance, and I can't remember anything about his features. He had too much goop on his face."

"That's okay. You're doing good. Now tell me what you know about Simon's death—the facts first, as you know them, then your own feelings and the reason you feel that way."

With as many details as she could remember, she

told him about her father's odd behavior the last few days before his death and the gun-permit request she'd found in his desk.

Dan didn't interrupt her. She had expected him to pull out a notebook and start taking notes the way the two uniformed officers had done the other night, or stop her and ask her to backtrack.

He did neither.

"Do you have any idea who would want to kill your father?" he asked when she was finished.

Jill slowly shook her head. "I must have asked myself that same question a hundred times, and I still can't come up with an answer. People adored him. He was kind, generous, enthusiastic about his work, and the work of others. Oh, he had his share of enemies. We all do, I suppose. But I doubt any of them would want to kill him."

"Can you be specific? About his enemies, I mean."

"That was only a figure of speech—"

"Think, Jill. We could be talking about a disgruntled former employee, a rival architect, a client."

Once again, she was surprised at the way he was able to draw information from her. "Well...there's Pete Mulligan."

"The building contractor?"

Jill nodded. "He hated my father. He wanted to go into a joint venture with B&A in the worst way but was never able to."

"Why not?"

"His bids were always too high, and my father never liked him, anyway. Six months ago, Mulligan came to B&A and accused my father of manipulating the bids and keeping him out of the bidding process.

My father was furious and threw him out of his office.''

Dan made a mental note to check on Pete Mulligan. ''Who else didn't get along with your father?''

''My cousin Olivia. She's always resented him for taking me under his wing years ago and for placing me in a position of power later on. Professionally, she fought with him all the time.''

''About what?''

''Money matters, management matters. You know Olivia, she always has something to say. More recently, she was upset because my father turned down a buyout offer from a big conglomerate. She thinks that merging with a large international company could help our bottom line.''

Dan's expression turned curious. ''Is B&A in financial trouble, Jill?''

''No. That's why my father wouldn't sell.'' Her voice tightened. ''It's different now, though. Clients are deserting us, afraid that without my father the company is doomed.''

''Tell me about the other board members.''

''You know them all.''

''It's been a while, Jill. Refresh my memory.''

''Well, beside Olivia, there's my uncle Cyrus. He's now the company president and I'm his vice president. The other two members are Paul Scoffield and Philip Van Horn.''

Dan remembered both men well. Scoffield was the company's financial officer and Van Horn headed B&A's legal department. ''Anything I should know about them?'' he asked. ''Money problems? Disagreements with your father?''

"Now that you mention it, Paul did have money problems. He made some bad investments after his wife died and almost lost his home. When my father found out, he loaned him enough money to get back on his feet."

Dan wasn't surprised at Simon's generosity. Jill's father had always been a great believer of spreading the wealth around. "Did Paul pay him back?"

"For the most part. I don't think Daddy was too worried about it."

"What about Philip?"

"No problems there. He and my father made a great team."

Her voice lost some of its crispness. "Poor Philip suffered a tragedy of his own not too long ago." She looked at Dan. "His daughter committed suicide."

"*Blair?*"

"Awful, isn't it? Such a happy, well-adjusted young woman."

"What happened?"

"She was attending law school at University of Pennsylvania in Philadelphia, and one night she jumped off the Ben Franklin Bridge. The following day, they found her body floating in the Delaware River."

"Christ."

"I know. Philip was devastated. All he found later was a note from Blair, but she didn't give an explanation. The note was to her father and all it said was 'Forgive me.'"

"The two of you were good friends, weren't you?"

"I was seven years older so she was more like my baby sister than a friend. After Philip and his wife divorced and Blair and her mother moved to Oklahoma, we sort of lost touch with each other, but I loved her very much.''

''What about the rest of the staff?'' Dan asked after a while.

''My father had no problem with anyone at B&A.'' A smile played on her lips. ''I doubt very much you're going to find a murderer in our midst, Dan.''

''Yet, someone at B&A eavesdropped on your conversation with your mother yesterday. And you said you felt as if you knew your attacker.''

''It wasn't someone I work with.''

Dan was thoughtful for a few minutes. Despite Jill's trust in her co-workers, he hadn't ruled out the possibility of an internal conflict. He put down his mug and, when she pointed at the coffeepot, he shook his head. ''How are the shares of the company divided?'' he asked.

''Before his death, my father had fifty-one shares, I had fifteen, Uncle Cyrus had nineteen. Olivia, Philip Van Horn and Paul Scoffield each had five. When my father died, my uncle inherited twenty of Daddy's shares and I the other thirty-one.''

''Nothing for your mother?''

''Daddy wanted his shares to go to Uncle Cy and me because we were involved in the business. Mom inherited everything else.'' Jill watched him for a moment. ''What do you think? Is it as hopeless as it seems?''

''Intriguing maybe, but not hopeless.''

''Where will you begin?''

''At the crash scene. I'll talk to Wally and get some specifics.'' He took his empty mug to the sink.

"Thanks for the brew, Red." He winked. "When did you learn to make such good coffee?"

"This cop I knew showed me how. I was married to him and had lots of time to practice while he was working."

The stab hit him hard. "I know I've said it before, Jill, but I'm sorry. About everything."

She shrugged. "Forget it. I have."

His gaze moved over her face, slowly, taking in every inch, lingering more than he should have on her lips. The effect was so unsettling she felt herself blush. "Why are you looking at me like that?"

"Because I can't believe I let you go."

He was close enough for her to smell his aftershave, a woodsy scent that suited him perfectly. *Easy girl. Don't let him get to you. One heartbreak was enough.*

Jill squared her shoulders. "Don't get any ideas, Santini. What we once had is over. Finito. You do understand that word, don't you?"

"Oh, I understand it." As she started to turn away, he took her chin between two fingers and turned her head back. For a wild moment, she thought he was going to kiss her. The sensation was so powerful, she could almost feel his mouth on hers. "Whether or not I believe it is another matter."

It was a while until she was able to regain her composure. When she did, she brushed his hand away. "Believe it."

Nine

"Oh, Jill, how could you?" Amanda waited until the couple seated at the next table had left before giving her daughter a long, reproachful look. "How could you ask a stranger to investigate your father's death, to pry into our lives, question us like...criminals."

Because Lutèce was always crowded at lunch hour and private conversations were seldom private, Jill leaned over the table and kept her voice low. "First of all, Dan is not going to treat you and the rest of the family like criminals. He's quite aware that you're grieving. Second, he's hardly a stranger. He was part of our family for an entire year."

Her duck terrine forgotten, Amanda's expression went from angry to startled. "Well, haven't you made a three-hundred-and-sixty-degree turnaround. I thought you hated the man's guts."

Jill held back a smile. The phrase, which sounded out of place coming from her mother, was one she had used herself many times following her separation from Dan. Looking back, she wasn't sure if she had said it to convince her parents she hated him or to convince herself. "Hate is a worthless emotion," she stated with a shrug.

"Dear God, don't tell me you're falling in love with

him again. Oh, Jill, that wouldn't be wise at all. You two are worlds apart. You've always been. And he's hurt you so much.''

"I hurt him, too, Mom."

Looking totally dismayed, Amanda leaned back against her chair. "You *have* fallen in love with him again!''

"No," Jill said in a fierce whisper. "I have *not*. If you want to know the truth, I wish Ashley had minded her own business and not called him. But she did call him, and, by God, I'm going to make the most of it. And after he's finished with this investigation, we'll both go our separate ways and I'll probably never see him again.''

"If you had to bring in an investigator, why did it have to be him?''

"Because he's good at what he does." Jill paused. "And because I trust him.''

Amanda let out a small, resigned sigh. "Since it's obvious I can't change your mind, I guess I might as well agree to talk to him. What exactly does he want to know?''

"He wants to reconstruct Daddy's last forty-eight hours. If that's not enough, he'll have to go back further.''

Her mouth still set in a tight, disapproving line, Amanda nodded. "All right, then. Tell him to come to the town house tomorrow morning at about ten. The sooner we do this the sooner you'll realize how wrong you are.''

"Thanks, Mom. I knew you'd come through for me." Withdrawing her hand, Jill took a bite of her own terrine. "Now eat your lunch." Her eyes filled with mischief. "I don't mind taking you out to one of the most expensive restaurants in town, but you have to eat the food."

Amanda's lips quivered slightly as if she was trying not to smile. "That's what *I* used to tell you."

"I know. Isn't it fun reversing roles once in a while?"

Amanda picked up her fork. "Just don't get used to it. I'm still your mother."

Jill smiled. "Yes, Mom."

Although Amanda Bennett had agreed to see Dan and answer his questions, her demeanor on Sunday morning was exactly as Dan had predicted—polite, cool and cautiously distant.

Unlike Simon, she had been against Jill marrying Dan from the start—not because of the young couple's social differences, but because she didn't think her impetuous daughter had the temperament to become a policeman's wife. And in that respect, she had been right.

Fortunately, Dan's visit to the Bennetts' town house hadn't been a total waste of time. Oddly enough, it wasn't what Amanda had told him that he'd found intriguing, but what she had *not* told him.

As he drove back to Brooklyn, the nagging feeling that she had been hiding something kept coming back, yet her account of Simon's last forty-eight hours was perfectly believable. On Saturday, he had gone to the office for a few hours, then had come home for an early dinner. Later he had retreated to his study, as he often did at night.

On Sunday, they and another couple had gone to

the Plaza Hotel for brunch. Afterward, Amanda had gone home to write her Christmas cards and Simon had driven to Livingston Manor, by himself. It was no secret that Amanda didn't share her husband's passion for the outdoors, especially in the winter.

So what could she have possibly not told Dan?

The question stayed with him until he reached his mother's house where the entire Santini clan had gathered for a big Sunday dinner. As his two nephews met him at the door with a football, challenging him to a quick game before dinner, he forgot about Amanda Bennett and headed for the backyard.

With a few strokes of her pencil, Jill put the finishing touches to her Church Hill sketch and pulled back from her drawing board for a look at what six weeks of intense work had accomplished.

The design of the sixty-four-story luxury-apartment complex had changed dramatically since she had first presented her idea to the Maitland Group two months ago. She'd replaced the angles, which she had thought too harsh, with gentle curves, and she'd added an additional wing to the structure, giving it a cloverleaf effect.

Because the new design was as unique and exciting as anything she had ever done, Jill had taken a gamble, hoping that Ben Maitland, a man who had a flair for the unusual, would like it. Now, as a serious case of jitters began to set in, she grew more and more fearful. What if she had misjudged him? What if Maitland hated the new design?

"May I come in?"

Recognizing the deep, baritone voice of Philip Van

Horn, Jill swung around in her chair, already smiling. "Of course."

Just under six foot and slender, Philip Van Horn was an attractive man with dark hair that was beginning to gray and probing, intelligent brown eyes. Except for a mild setback shortly after his daughter's death, he hadn't allowed his grief to interfere with his work. Under his leadership, B&A's legal department was running as smoothly as ever.

"I thought I'd stop by to wish you luck in Richmond," he said. Standing beside Jill, he let his gaze skim the sketches and he shook his head in wonder. "I'm not an architect but I can see why Cyrus insisted I take a look at these."

Jill beamed with pride. "You really like them?"

"Like them? Jill, this is a fabulous concept. One look at this building and Ben Maitland won't be able to turn it down."

"Thank you, Philip." Jill started rolling up the drawings. "To tell you the truth, I'm a little nervous. So much rests on this presentation."

"You'll do fine," Philip said with a confidence that restored some of her own. "When will you be back?"

She hesitated but only briefly. "This evening. I didn't want to run the risk of having to cut my meeting short, so I booked a later flight." There was no reason to tell him, or anyone at B&A, any more than that.

"Let us know how it went as soon as you get a chance."

"All right. Just don't pop the Dom Pérignon without me, will you?"

Philip laughed. "I wouldn't dream of it."

She was sliding the drawings into a tube when her

secretary rang her on the intercom. "Your taxi is here, Jill."

"Thanks, Cathie. Tell the driver I'll be right down."

The tube in one hand and her purse slung over her shoulder, Jill said a hasty goodbye to Philip, who gave her the thumbs-up sign, and was off.

Except for a couple slouched in the front row and the two actors on the brilliantly lit stage, the Aquarius Theater on Forty-third Street was empty.

The male actor, a short, portly man in a goatee, was reading from a script, while Lilly Grant, the star of *One Night In Paris,* delivered her lines from memory and with great panache. She wore comfortable pants in a muted shade of brown and a cream blouse. Her brown hair was gathered on top of her head in a rather unruly knot à la Katharine Hepburn. It was a look she had been perfecting for years and it suited her to a tee.

Amanda Bennett's sister had always been one of Dan's favorite people. Broadway's most legendary leading lady for almost forty years, she hadn't let fame and fortune go to her head, and while acting was an integral part of her, and one never really knew when she wasn't acting, she was warm, funny and undeniably charming.

Hands in his pockets, Dan walked quietly down the aisle. At the fourth row, he took a seat and leaned back, smiling as the woman on the stage struck a theatrical pose.

"How low of you, Harland," she said in that same deep, compelling voice that had delighted audiences for the past four decades. "How despicably low and cowardly of you to remind me of my failings. Have I not suffered enough? Repented enough?''

"Harland" took a puff of his cigar and let out a small snort. "Repent? You? My dear Finiola, I don't think you even know the meaning of the word." As he took another puff, he was suddenly overcome by a raging coughing spell.

In the front row, the man Dan assumed was the director threw his script in the air and jumped out of his seat. "Jesus Christ, Michael," he bellowed. "What the hell is it now? First you screw up your lines, then you knock down the props, and now this. Are we ever going to get through this scene without an interruption? This is a Broadway play, people, not a kindergarten production. And in case you forgot, we open in three weeks."

"It's this damn cigar." The actor threw the culprit on the floor and stomped on it like a spoiled child. "I told you I can't stomach this domestic stuff. Get me something decent, will you? Like a Havana."

"Havanas are illegal, Michael."

"I don't give a shit. Get them." His head held high, Michael stormed off the stage.

"Michael, come back here." The director and his assistant hurried after him. "You know the play can't go on without you."

Lilly Grant, never one to miss a grand moment, placed a hand on her hip as her gaze followed the disappearing trio. "The show can't go on without him? What am I? Chopped liver? Wasn't *my* performance good enough to warrant even one compliment?"

Rising from his seat, Dan began clapping, slowly at

first, then with more vigor as he made his way toward the stage. "You were magnificent, Miss Grant, superb, scintillating. Bravo!"

Obviously pleased, Lilly Grant squinted toward the dark theater. "Thank you, young man." The exasperation was gone from her voice but not the drama. "Come up here, will you?" She waved him closer. "Your voice sounds familiar. Have we met?"

"Out of sight out of mind, Lilly?" Dan's voice was gently teasing. "Shame on you. And you claimed to have such a crush on me."

"Daniel?" Clear, seductive laughter cascaded from her lips like a bubbling brook. As Dan climbed the steps to the stage, Lilly's hands flew to her mouth. "It *is* you."

"In the flesh, Lilly."

Raising herself on tiptoe, she kissed him European style, on both cheeks. "Amanda told me you were in town." Holding him at arm's length, the actress gave him a long appraising look. "You scoundrel, you haven't changed a bit. You're still as handsome as ever."

"And you're still the most beautiful, most talented stage actress in the world."

Lilly struck another theatrical pose. "Then, will you tell me why they have paired me with this whining, boring, second-rate performer who has the nerve to call himself an actor? The man never stops complaining, he has the personality of an old prune and about as much stage presence."

Dan chuckled. Lilly had never been one to mince words.

Seductive again, she gazed at him beneath long, dark lashes. "How long have you been watching?"

"Long enough to want to see more."

She had the grace to blush, another of the many tricks of the trade Lilly Grant had mastered over the years. Dan did some quick math. She had to be well over sixty, maybe closer to sixty-five, yet she was still considered one of the world's great beauties. Petite and slender, she had the most extraordinary slanted green eyes, a thin but well-defined mouth and impossibly high cheekbones.

She gave him a coy look. "And you really thought I was good?"

Knowing how much she liked compliments, Dan bowed his head. "You were brilliant. I predict you'll bring the house down on opening night."

"From your lips to God's ears."

"Amanda told me you toured for almost four months."

"Six cities in twelve weeks. Two hundred and sixteen performances."

"And I bet every one of them got a standing ovation."

She flashed him a dazzling smile. "The play, thank God, was an uncontested hit. Not only did we have standing ovations and packed houses, but the reviews were fabulous." She laughed. "I even received three marriage proposals."

"You were always a heartbreaker, Lilly."

"Let's go find a seat." Lilly extended her hand to Dan so he could escort her off the stage. "You and I have some catching up to do, though I don't know how much time we'll have. Michael's tantrums have been known to last anywhere between three minutes and three days.''

When they were seated in the front row, she turned toward him. "Amanda told me you came to New York to investigate Simon's death."

"That's right."

"I don't think she's too happy about it."

"She made that abundantly clear."

"I can't say I blame her. To suddenly find out your husband may have been murdered must be rather unsettling.'' Leaning back, she draped her left arm over the backrest. "But for my part, I'm glad you're here. I don't see you nearly as often as I'd like." The famous green eyes glinted with amusement. "I'd love to hear what my lovely niece had to say when she saw you."

Dan smiled. "She didn't throw anything at me if that's what you mean, though I have a feeling she may have wanted to."

Lilly's clear laughter echoed through the empty theater. "Well, you must have done something right to make her come around so quickly, and I'm glad. She may not show it, but her father's death affected her greatly."

"It couldn't have been too easy for you, either, dealing with your sister's grief and preparing for your Broadway opening."

"I was devastated," Lilly said dramatically. "Oh, sure, Simon and I had our differences, but who doesn't in a diversified family such as ours?"

"He wasn't much of a theater fan, if I recall."

"No." A shadow seemed to pass over her beautiful features. "He thought that grown-ups standing on a stage pretending to be something they weren't was hogwash. Still, he came to every one of my opening nights."

"Were you touring when he died?"

"Thank God, no, I was already back in New York. Rehearsals had just begun." Glancing toward the stage, she waved. "Luke, darling, come here. I want you to meet someone."

As Luke approached, Dan stood up and Lilly made the introductions. "Luke, this is Dan Santini, formerly of the NYPD and one of my dearest friends. Dan, meet my talented director, Luke Mansfield. And this lovely lady here is his assistant, Lisa, who ought to be given a medal for putting up with all of us eighteen hours a day."

The two men shook hands. "NYPD, huh?" Mansfield squinted at him. "What department did you work in?"

"Homicide. I was a detective."

"Not just a detective," Lilly interjected, "but one of the best in the country. He's the one who cracked the Barnaby case a few years ago."

"The serial killer?" Mansfield seemed impressed.

"I wasn't working alone," Dan said, realizing how much he still hated the limelight. "Catching Barnaby was a team effort."

"Knowing what I know about the man, you and your team have my deepest admiration. Now, if you don't mind, I have to go find some imported cigars before our temperamental leading man has another fit. Nice to've met you, Dan. Come and see us on opening night, will you?"

"I wouldn't miss it."

Lilly stood up. "I guess I'd better go see how Michael is doing. If he doesn't snap out of this mood, we'll be rehearsing until three o'clock in the morning." Kissing Dan's cheek, she added, "Come back for a full rehearsal as soon as you have a chance." The green eyes sparkled. "And bring Jill with you. I want to see if the two of you still look as good together as you used to."

"Now, Lilly, don't get any ideas."

"I'll get all the ideas I want. You and Jill were a perfect match. You may not have known it at the time, but I sure did. When the two of you entered a room, you could almost feel the chemistry. It was magical."

She laid delicate fingers on his arm. "Speaking of magic, do you still…"

Quick as lightning, Dan's hand shot out, touched Lilly's ear and came back holding a ruby ring. "I believe this is yours."

Her mouth forming a perfect O, Lilly glanced at her left hand. "My ruby. How did you do that?" She looked up, her expression one of pure delight. "I never felt it leaving my finger."

Dan slid the ring back. "Just call me Merlin." He kissed her again. "I'll see you soon, Lilly."

Ten

Of the many presentations Jill had made over the last six years, none had meant more to her than the one she was about to make in front of Ben Maitland and his five partners.

Not only was this new commission a turning point in her career, it would be the first project she would complete on her own, without her father's guidance and supervision.

Now, as she stood next to the easel where she had propped up her drawings, some of her earlier confidence began to slip. She thought she knew those six men, knew what they expected of her, knew the image they were trying to project. But as she looked at their sober faces, she was as uncertain as she had been on the day of her very first presentation.

At last, she took a deep breath, said a silent prayer and flipped the cover sheet over, exposing the first sketch—a rendition of the entire building.

Almost immediately, the six men gravitated forward, as if pulled by an invisible force. Their eyebrows seemed to knit in unison and their expressions, though still serious, were no longer as intimidating.

Jill held back a sigh of relief. She had their attention.

Resisting the need to clear her throat, she forged ahead. "When we first met two months ago," she began, "the concept was to build a rather angular tower, a structure reminiscent of the Transamerica Pyramid in San Francisco, or the First Interstate Bank Tower in Dallas. As I began working on the preliminary designs, however, I realized that none of them reflected the uniqueness you gentlemen were trying to achieve. None were saying to me, 'Here I am,' and none had the potential to become a world-famous landmark.

"This building does," she continued, turning to look at her sketch. "As you can see, I've softened the lines, and I've added one more wing so as to create a cloverleaf effect." As she talked, she ran her pointer up and down the broad curves of the building. "This will achieve a double purpose. It eliminates the treatment of corners—where one wall abuts another—and it maximizes privacy."

"How so?" Ben Maitland asked.

Again, Jill's pointer skimmed over the design. "Because the one-hundred-twenty-degree angles of the building make it virtually impossible for one neighbor to peek at another. And because of the unique triform shape, every apartment will have a view of James River."

She could tell by the way the six men slowly nodded that they knew exactly what that meant. An apartment with a view would sell at twice the price. Encouraged, she moved her pointer up a notch. "At the very top of the building, the rounded effect continues with a circular roof garden and enough space for private parties or informal gatherings. As agreed, the building will also include an underground garage and a complete recreational facility.''

"That extra wing is going to increase costs dramatically,'' Jerome Tippin remarked.

"Yes, but it will also give you an additional two hundred units, and based on your projections and our own market research of the area, those extra apartments will be snapped up in no time and will more than offset the extra cost.''

"She's right,'' Ben said, turning to his financial officer. "This city is experiencing tremendous urban renewal. Young professionals are moving back to town and affluent baby boomers whose children have moved out of the nest are looking for a less complicated life-style. I agree with Jill. We won't have any problem selling those extra units.''

Another partner nodded. "I feel the same way.''

Ben turned back to Jill. "Let's take a look at what you've done with the apartments.''

Finding it difficult to hold back her excitement, Jill flipped the page and continued her presentation.

By the time she was finished, shortly after two o'clock, all six partners had reversed their earlier decision and were as eager as she was to begin the project. They even apologized for what they called their shortsightedness and lack of faith.

An hour and a half later, Jill was landing at Washington National Airport. With her commuter flight to New York not leaving until five-thirty, she had almost two hours to find out if someone remembered seeing her father.

Outside the terminal, she approached a skycap. "I

wonder if you could help me," she said pleasantly. "I'm trying to locate this man."

Opening her purse, she took out a five-by-seven photograph of her father and showed it to him. "He landed here on the morning of October 3. I'm fairly sure he would have needed a cab."

The man didn't even look at the photograph. "Sorry, miss. I didn't start working until Thanksgiving Day." He nodded toward a lanky, white-haired African-American. "But Tyrone over there should be able to help you." He chuckled. "He's been here since the airplane was invented."

Tyrone was a busy man and Jill had to wait for nearly fifteen minutes until the rush for cabs and hotel shuttles quieted down before she could talk to him. As he gallantly tipped his hat to her, she repeated her story, showing him her father's picture and discreetly sliding a fifty-dollar bill into his hand.

Surprised, he looked at the money, but didn't put it away.

"I remember him," he said as he studied the picture. "He was a good tipper, just like you. But not much of a talker, so I can't tell you where he went. He asked me to get him a cab, tipped me and that was it."

"Do you remember the name of the cab company?"

"'Fraid not. It gets pretty busy here at that time of the morning, and there must be more than a dozen cab companies in this town. You could try D.C. Taxi Service, though. They're the biggest."

"I will." Jill handed him her card. "In the meantime, keep the photograph. If you find out whose cab my father took and where he went, there's another fifty in it for you. And the same for the cabdriver who supplies the information.''

''Mighty generous of you, miss. I'll certainly do my best.'' He tucked the card and the photograph in his pocket and touched his hat again before turning to greet another group of travelers.

Re-entering the terminal, Jill went to the nearest public phone, opened the phone book that lay on a narrow shelf and flipped through it, stopping at the taxi section. Tyrone had not exaggerated. The listings for the Washington, Virginia and Maryland area occupied four pages. Ignoring the quick pang of guilt, she neatly ripped out each one of them, shoved them into her purse and went out to hail a cab.

At first, the dispatcher at D.C. Taxi Service, a woman by the name of Delilah, was reluctant to talk to her. Cab companies, she stated, especially in this town, didn't like to get embroiled in intrigue. Aware that she wouldn't get anywhere with lies, Jill opted to tell her as much of the truth as she possibly could, explaining that her father had died and she was trying to locate a relative Simon had visited during his Washington trip on October 3.

Producing another photo of her father's, and another fifty-dollar bill, she asked Delilah if she would please circulate the picture among her drivers. As she talked, Jill slid the fifty across the woman's desk. This time, the bill was snapped up by chubby, bejeweled fingers and quickly disappeared.

''I'll see what I can do,'' Delilah said as a call to dispatch a cab to the Mayflower Hotel came through.

Jill repeated the process with two other cab companies. She would have squeezed in a third, but was out of time and had to get back to the airport.

Her plane was already boarding when she reached her gate.

There was only one private investigator in New York City Dan trusted implicitly and that was Al Metzer, the same man he would have recommended to Jill, had he been sure she would have hired him.

A former marine surveillance expert in Vietnam, Al had opened his downtown agency in the late seventies and made a name for himself by handling a variety of cases ranging from arson to missing persons and a little bit of everything in between. The firm now employed fifteen operatives and was one of the most reliable and trusted detective agencies on the East Coast.

The two men had met during Dan's first year as a homicide detective and, in spite of their occasional opposing views regarding some of the cases they were working on, Dan had a great deal of respect for the older man.

Average in every way, Al was the perfect P.I., as much at ease in a suit and tie as he was in a pair of chinos and a baseball hat. He could change appearance in the blink of an eye and be forgotten just as quickly, which suited him just fine.

He had made only one transformation in recent years—a discreet brown toupee to cover his balding head, which he claimed made him too memorable.

His office was, as always, a mess. Photos of army buddies shared wall space with various Manhattan landscapes, a small glass cabinet was crammed with bowling trophies and his desk bulged with case files. More files were stacked on the floor against one wall.

"What you need," Dan commented as he looked around him, "is a bigger office—something the size of Shea Stadium maybe?"

Al dismissed the suggestion with a wave of his hand. "That would only encourage me to accumulate more junk." He removed his briefcase from a chair so Dan could sit down. "It's been a while since I've seen you. You came to spend the holidays with the family?"

"I wish it were that simple."

"Ah." Al handed him a cup of coffee Dan knew would curl his toes. He was not disappointed.

"I have a job for you, if you're interested."

"I'm all ears."

"Does the name Pete Mulligan mean anything to you?"

Al took a noisy slurp. "Junior or senior?"

"Junior."

"I know he took over his father's company a couple of years ago."

"What else can you tell me about him?"

"He's not as reliable as the old man was, or as ethical. There's also a nasty rumor that he may have ties with the Mob."

"I want to know everything you can find out about the man, Al, including where he was on the night of December 1."

Al noted the information on a yellow pad. "I'll put an operative on it right away. What happened on the night of December 1?"

"That's when Simon Bennett died. You knew him, didn't you?"

Al nodded. "Sure, he was your ex-father-in-law. His car went off the road somewhere in the Catskill Mountains."

"It's possible his death wasn't an accident, after all."

Al's interest perked up considerably. "And you think Mulligan did it?"

"Let's just say it's a possibility." Dan told hir what he knew about the relationship between the tv men.

Al took a few more notes. "All right, let's see v we can find out about Junior."

Dan jotted down his mother's phone number business card and gave it to Al. "You can rea there. Or on my cell phone." From his breast Dan pulled out a check. "Here's a thousand-d tainer. Anything above that, bill me at my address."

Al waved his hand. "I don't need a ret you, Dan. We've been friends too long done me too many favors in the past—"

Dan had expected this reaction and for it. "Take the retainer, Al, or we d ness."

With a small sigh, Al took the che a drawer. "All right. I know better th a hardhead like you."

"You're a wise man." Standing paper cup into the trash. "I've got as soon as you hear something."

At the door, he turned around. "By the way, I never got a chance to tell you before, but I like the new do."

Crumpling a piece of paper, Al threw it at him. Laughing, Dan caught the makeshift ball in midair, threw it back at the detective and closed the door.

Eleven

After leaving Al's office, Dan drove straight to the small hamlet of Livingston Manor in Sullivan County where he had made arrangements to meet Constable Wally Becker.

A stone's throw from Manhattan, this rugged wilderness on the southeastern corner of New York State had become a refuge for weary New Yorkers and boasted some of the most famous trout streams in the United States. It was here, knee-deep in the Beaverkill River, that Simon had taught Dan the art of fly-fishing and made him forget, at least temporarily, that he had just lost his father.

Pushing the memories aside, Dan followed Wally's directions to Johnston Road until he reached the bend where Simon's Jeep had gone off the road. After getting out of the car, he walked to the edge of the cliff, where a shiny ten-foot section of the guardrail had already been replaced. Rock and charred brush where the car had burned lined the valley floor, a stark reminder of the inferno that had taken place there.

Stepping over the railing, Dan walked down a narrow path, covering the two-hundred-feet distance in a little over five minutes. Hands in his pockets, he walked around the crash site, searching for evidence he knew wouldn't be there. Wally was much too thorough to have left anything of significance behind.

Satisfied he wouldn't find anything, Dan made the climb back. Twenty minutes later, he was being shown into Wally's town-hall office.

"Here you are," Wally said as he came around his desk to greet him. "I was beginning to wonder if one of our mountain bears had come out of hibernation and gobbled you up."

Laughing, Dan took the offered hand and shook it. "The only mountain bear I have to watch for is right here, in a fancy uniform." He clasped Wally's thick arm. "You're looking good, my friend."

"It's all that fresh mountain air." Wally pushed his chest out and tapped it a few times as if to prove the fullness of his lungs. "There's no better antidote for old age. You ought to try it some time."

"I'll keep that in mind—when I reach old age."

"Don't be so cocky, boy, you'll get there soon enough."

After a few seconds of silence, Wally smoothed down his thick mustache, a habit he had when he was about to discuss something unpleasant. "You stopped at the crash site?"

Dan nodded. "There wasn't much to see."

"I told you." Wally walked back to his desk and opened a drawer. "I have some photographs that were taken the night of the accident and the morning after when we hauled up the car. I didn't show them to the family but you're welcome to take a look at them."

Wally handed Dan a stack of eight-by-ten glossies. "I warn you, though. It's pretty gruesome stuff."

Dan looked at the photographs, twelve in all, and

understood why Wally hadn't showed them to Simon's family. The Jeep's windows were blown out from the explosion, the leather seats in shreds, the metal frame black and twisted. The driver's door, torn from its hinges, lay on the ground several feet from the Jeep. Simon's body, such as it was, sat in the front seat, a charred mass Dan wouldn't have recognized as human.

It was a while until Dan could talk again. "Who reported the accident?"

"Old Newt Brentworth. A stray cat got into his hardware store, tripping the burglar alarm, and Newt had to drive to town to check it out. He was on his way back home when he saw the flames. The state police got there first and then they called me. Even with the heavy rain, the car was still burning when the fire department arrived."

"Why such a big fire? The gas tanks in those Jeeps are rather small, aren't they?"

"That's right, but Simon had an auxiliary tank installed a year or so ago. I told him that was a bad idea, but he wouldn't listen. A week earlier he had run out of gas in the middle of nowhere and had to walk five miles before he found a gas station. He swore that would never happen again."

Dan put the last photograph down. "Where's the Jeep now?"

"At Marcus's junkyard on Route 28. Amanda told him to sell it for scrap. I've checked it out pretty thoroughly, but if you want to take a look at it, I'll be glad to take you there."

"I'd appreciate that." Then, because he wanted to make sure he wasn't stepping on any toes or hurting

Wally's feelings, he added, "You don't mind my butting in, do you?"

"Hell, no. And you're not butting in. As I told you earlier, I closed the case. To tell you the truth, I'm glad you're here. Your ex-wife is one stubborn young woman and I was beginning to worry about her." He put the photographs back in the drawer. "So if there's anything I can do to make your job easier, just holler, okay?"

"Thanks, Wally."

Wally watched Dan for a while. "Are you doing this just to make Jill happy? Or do you honestly believe Simon was murdered?"

"It's too early to tell yet, but I must admit there are enough discrepancies in this case to pique my curiosity." Dan pushed his chair back and stood up. "So if it's all right with you, I'd like to take a look at the summer house."

"Sure. As a matter of fact, Amanda called to say you'd probably want to do that." He rummaged through another drawer. "I have Joshua's keys here somewhere."

"Who's Joshua?"

"Oh, that's right, you've never met him. He's the caretaker at the Bennetts' house. He does a little bit of everything, picks up the mail, keeps an eye on the house when it's empty, shovels the driveway, that sort of thing."

"Does he live on the property?"

Wally nodded. "In a small log cabin a couple of hundred feet from the main house."

"Is he there now?"

"Nope. He's spending a few days with an old aunt.

He should be back at the end of the week. I already questioned him, though. He was home that night but didn't see or hear anything.''

"I'd still like to talk to him.''

"I'll let you know when he gets back. Ah, here they are.'' He held up a set of keys. "Why don't we go to the junkyard first? Marcus goes to lunch promptly at noon and, depending on how many Buds he's had with his burger, he won't reopen until he sobers up.'' He chuckled. "That could be three days from now.''

From a nail on the wall, Wally unhooked a heavily lined jacket the same dark blue shade as his pants and slipped it on. "Let's go.''

As Dan had expected, the burned hulk of Simon's Jeep held no evidence of tampering. After thanking Marcus, who, judging from the way he kept looking at his watch, was getting thirsty, Dan and Wally got back in the Land Rover and headed toward the Bennetts' house, which stood at the top of Johnston Road.

The three-story structure was a contemporary masterpiece. Built on a sloped, heavily wooded two-hundred-acre lot and made entirely of cedar and glass, it afforded a spectacular view from each of the four exposures.

Simon had spared no expense. From the floating balcony cantilevered over the living/dining area, to the huge retractable skylight and soaring stone fireplace, the house was a perfect union of function, flow and formidable beauty.

"I've been in this house dozens of times,'' Wally said, "and each time I'm in awe.''

"Simon was never one to do things in a small way."

Dan's gaze came back to the fireplace. The fluffy white throw rug was still there, a gut-stirring reminder of another cold winter afternoon when he and Jill had lain naked in front of a roaring fire and made love well into the night.

"That's the bottle we found." Unaware of Dan's momentary distraction, Wally nodded at a triangular-shaped teak bar opposite the fireplace. Behind it, three glass shelves held an impressive assortment of scotches, bourbons and after-dinner liquors. On the counter stood a half-filled bottle of Chivas Regal.

"Any prints on it?"

"Only Simon's. Same with the glass."

Dan opened the bottle of single malt and sniffed the contents.

"We tested it," Wally said. "There was nothing in there but pure scotch. My guess is that Simon drank quite a bit of it before he left."

"Why do you say that?"

"There was liquor splashed on the bar top, next to the glass and on the rug—though it's been cleaned up since then—suggesting that his coordination was less than perfect."

"Was anything disturbed? Furniture toppled over?"

"If you mean, was there any sign of a struggle, the answer is no. The place was just as neat and clean as you see it now."

Silently, Dan walked around the room, inspecting the thick tan carpet, the deep burgundy sofas, the baby grand, the fireplace that smelled of hickory wood. A set of heavy brass andirons stood on each side of the stone hearth. He picked one up and inspected it closely, turning it around several time, paying particular attention to the heavy base and the ball-tipped end. He did the same with the other, then directed his attention to the fireplace poker. Wally was right. Everything was scrupulously clean.

"Did Simon ever bring anyone here outside of the family?" Dan asked. "I know he loved to fish and hunt, but I don't recall either Amanda or Jill sharing his passion."

"As far as I know, his brother and I were the only ones who came here on a regular basis, but I could be wrong. Simon didn't always tell me when he was coming up." He peered out the large window that overlooked a thick cluster of hemlock trees. "If I had known he was at the summer house that Sunday, I would have stopped by, and who knows? I might have been able to talk him into spending the night here."

"Don't blame yourself for Simon's death, Wally. You'll go crazy if you do. You weren't his keeper."

"I know, I know," Wally grumbled.

With the constable at his side, Dan went through the rest of the house and gave it a quick but thorough inspection.

"We dusted the entire house," Wally volunteered as Dan went from room to room. "We also checked the pool, the spa and the gazebo. Most of the prints there belonged to Simon. Others belonged to members of his family, Joshua, who has access to the house, the cleaning lady and myself."

There was nothing here, Dan thought as he made his way down the broad staircase, no clues, no evidence, nothing that could substantiate Jill's suspicions.

Wally and his men had come to the only conclusion they could have reached under the circumstances. If Jill hadn't been so adamant in her beliefs, Dan would have accepted the accidental-death theory as readily as Wally had.

"Thanks, my friend," Dan said as the two men got back into the Land Rover. "You were a great help."

"No need to thank me. I'd reopen the case myself in a second if I could justify my action to my superiors." Reaching behind him, Wally took hold of his seat belt and pulled it across his chest. "Let me know what you find out, will you?" he asked. "Because if someone really did kill Simon, nothing would please me more than to have the son of a bitch all to myself for just five minutes."

Twelve

Dressed in navy leggings, a blue denim shirt and thick white socks gathered at the ankles, Jill stood in front of her pantry, debating what to have for dinner. With her lack of culinary skills, the choice was limited, and not terribly exciting—a can of soup or a bowl of cereal.

She was reaching for the Corn Flakes when the door bell rang, followed by Dan's voice calling out her name.

"I thought I'd bring you up-to-date on the day's events," Dan said, walking in the moment she opened the door. "Maybe over dinner?"

"I don't think so."

"Oh, come on. That little French bistro you and I discovered years ago is still there. Why don't we see if the pot-au-feu is as good as it used to be?"

Being alone with Dan in a candlelit restaurant with romantic French music piping through the speakers was the last thing Jill wanted right now. "I'm too tired to go out."

"Okay. We'll eat here." Before she could ask him what he meant by that, he had removed his jacket and thrown it on the back of a chair. "You won't even have to lift a finger."

"*You're* going to cook?"

"Why the look of surprise? This is the nineties, you know. Men are no longer helpless in the kitchen. Especially unmarried men."

She had often wondered why he hadn't remarried, but didn't ask. She didn't want to give him the impression she cared. "I'm afraid you won't find anything even remotely resembling a dinner in my refrigerator. I'm a big believer in takeout."

"You'd be amazed at how resourceful I can be when properly motivated." He made a big production of rolling up his sleeves. When he was done, he pointed to the refrigerator. "May I?"

She shrugged, watching him as he pulled the door open and inspected the contents of her white, side-by-side G.E. "Hmm, let's see. We have a handful of mushrooms, not in the best condition but they'll do, half an onion, a loaf of bread, butter and... What's that?" he asked, lifting the corner of a foil-wrapped package and sniffing it.

"Anchovy pizza." She fought hard to hold back a smile. "I'm not sure how long the poor thing's been incarcerated."

Holding the package at arm's length, he handed it to her. "In that case, why don't we put it out of its misery and see what we can do with what we've got." He carried his meager selection to the kitchen counter. "You got any rice? Arborio preferably."

She looked in a cabinet. "Will Uncle Ben do?"

"In a pinch." Gently pushing her aside, he glanced inside the pantry. In no time at all, he had located a bottle of olive oil, a package of bouillon cubes and a can of Parmesan cheese. "How did it go in Richmond?"

"Great. The Maitland Group was impressed and we're rehired."

"Then we'll make this a celebration dinner." Glancing at the wine rack, he selected a bottle of Châteuneuf du Pape and handed it to her. "That used to be our favorite."

"Really?" She tried to sound innocent. "I don't remember." Why was she lying? So she liked the same wine they used to drink. Big deal. "I thought you were supposed to tell me about *your* day."

As he washed, chopped and sautéed, Dan told Jill about his visit with Lilly and his trip to Livingston Manor. "What can you tell me about Joshua?" he asked as he threw a handful of rice into the melted butter.

She frowned. "Why? You can't possibly think of him as a suspect."

"Sherlock Holmes once said that the quickest way to solve a crime was to eliminate the impossible until you were left with the improbable. That's what I'm doing."

"Then you can eliminate Joshua right away. He loved my father."

"How long has he been working for your family?"

"Five years. He used to work for one of Uncle Cyrus's friends. When Elliot died, Joshua found himself without a job. The state placed him in a—"

Dan turned around, a wooden spoon in his hand. "Hold it. Backtrack a little. Did you say the *state?*"

"Didn't Wally tell you? Joshua is, oh, how can I put it? Mentally challenged." So Dan wouldn't get the wrong impression, she quickly added, "He's also dependable, hardworking and loyal. His only family is an aunt who's too old to take care of him, so the state had to put him in a halfway house. When my uncle heard about it, he took Joshua to meet my father. Daddy hired him on the spot."

"And he let him live in his cabin?"

"It was nothing but a dilapidated shack at the time. My father bought what was needed to fix it up and let Joshua and a couple of handymen from the village do the rest." She smiled. "You should see it now. It looks like a little Hansel and Gretel cottage."

"Has he ever shown signs of violence?"

"Oh, for God's sake. Haven't you heard a word I said? Joshua is harmless." Reaching inside a cabinet, she took out two dishes and set them on the kitchen table with a bang. "And he's certainly not violent."

"I'm only trying to get a mental picture of the man, Jill, not crucify him," Dan said.

"Well, you're barking up the wrong tree."

Serious again, he said, "Maybe so, but your father wasn't killed by a stranger, that much I'm sure of. Whoever went after him knew Simon was at the Catskills house that night. He waited for him, the way he waited for you on MacDougal Street."

"And that's another reason why Joshua couldn't have done it. He'd never come to New York. All that noise and traffic would terrify him."

She watched as Dan stirred a handful of Parmesan cheese into the rice mixture before transferring the contents of the pot into a serving dish. "And you can't question him the way you would someone else. He's very shy, you see, especially around strangers, and he still hasn't recovered from my father's death."

"He talked to Wally, didn't he?"

"That's because he knows him. It would be different with you. He would be scared and I don't want that."

"Why don't you come with me when I go up, then? For your peace of mind. And if I screw up, you have my permission to punish me, any way you like." Glancing at her over his shoulder, he moved his eyebrows up and down a few times, Groucho Marx–style. "How's that?"

"Better."

"Good. Now let's eat."

Suddenly famished, she took the platter from him. "Mushroom risotto? I'm impressed."

"That was the idea."

She knew that wasn't true. For all his complexity, Dan was a simple man who never worried too much about what others thought of him. And he never tried to impress. Quite the contrary, he hated it when attention was focused on him.

They ate in silence for a few minutes. From time to time, Jill darted quick glances at him, amazed at his easy confidence, at the way he filled the room, as if he had never left it.

She shook the disturbing thought away. "Tell me about your life as a professor," she said. "Is it everything you thought it would be?"

"I'm only an associate professor," he corrected. "But yes, it's a very rewarding job. No two days are ever alike." He glanced at her. "How did you know I was teaching?"

"My mother and your mother keep in touch. Is Glenwood a large college?"

"A small one, but with a large enough endowment to allow courses other schools don't offer."

Jill took another bite of her risotto, which was excellent. His culinary talent was no surprise to her and his willingness to take over the duties of cook had certainly come in handy during their short marriage. Before she could stop it, the memory of the day he had tried to teach her how to flip pancakes brought a smile to her lips. She had flipped a little too hard and had sent the pancake flying onto the floor.

"What's so funny?"

She shook her head as if coming out of a dream. "What?"

"You were smiling just now."

"Oh. No reason." Jill took another bite of her food. "What exactly is applied criminal psychology?"

"Simply put?" He poured them both another glass of wine. "The study of the criminal mind."

"Are all your students future cops?"

"No." He laughed. "No one wants to be a cop anymore. My students are hoping to become criminal attorneys. This course will give them an advantage other attorneys don't have."

"You know, I wasn't all that surprised to hear you'd become a teacher. You always had a knack for making people listen to you."

His eyes filled with mirth. "Present company included?"

The remark lured another smile to her mouth. "I listened. Occasionally."

She pushed a slice of mushroom around with her

fork. The wine had mellowed her, making her feel relaxed, almost...happy. "You never remarried."

It was more a statement than a question and she regretted it the moment the words were out of her mouth. Whatever had possessed her to say that? Besides a burning curiosity.

"Neither did you." Dan's eyes made a slow, searching inspection of her face. "How come?"

She shrugged. "Too busy with my career."

"But there must have been..."

"Men?" She picked up her glass and studied the wine's ruby color for a second or two. "There were a few."

"Nothing serious I take it." He said it almost too casually.

"Oh, don't look so smug. And don't think for one moment that I kept comparing those men to you only to find they didn't measure up."

He feigned innocence. "Why, Jill, the thought never crossed my mind. Seriously, why didn't you remarry?"

She tore off a piece of bread from the slice on the edge of her plate and chewed it slowly. "To borrow a man's favorite expression, maybe I'm not the marrying kind."

"Or maybe," he said, "you never gave marriage a chance."

"Maybe." How could she tell him that the day their marriage broke up, a little piece of her heart had broken along with it? That she had never wanted to fall in love again? "Your turn, Professor. Why didn't *you* remarry?"

"That's easy. I never found anyone I wanted to

spend the rest of my life with, the way I'd hoped to do with you.''

Jill's eyes widened in surprise. Brought up in a mostly male Italian family, Dan had always been fiercely protective of his feelings, as if exposing them would somehow make him less of a man. "If you felt that way, why didn't you try to keep me?"

The bantering tone faded from his voice. "I did try to keep you. You weren't interested."

"How would you know? You were always angry, always walking out of the house."

"Maybe if you hadn't made your money such an issue, I wouldn't have been so angry."

They realized what they were doing simultaneously. Dan was the first to speak. "I'm sorry," he said. "That was a stupid thing for me to say."

"I guess this tête-à-tête was a bad idea, after all." Jill's tone was stiff, her back rigid as she stood up, gathered their plates and carried them to the sink.

Dan rose to his feet as well. "Jill, come on. You know I didn't mean to be critical. It's just—"

"It's just that we can't be in the same room five minutes together without being at each other's throats. And that will never change." She brushed by him as she returned to the table to pick up their glasses. "Why don't you leave before we find something else to fight about. It's late, anyway."

"Let me help you with the dishes."

"No." She froze him with a look. "Contrary to what you may think, there are *some* things I'm able to do by myself."

She stood at the window, watching him walk down MacDougal Street in his long easy stride. They should have never discussed their personal lives. If they were going to get along in this odd partnership, she would have to keep their relationship on a purely business level. And that meant no personal questions, no reference to the past and absolutely no cosy tête-à-têtes, with or without mushroom risotto.

By the time Dan reached the end of the block, where he had parked the Land Rover, her anger had vanished and the only words she could remember were those he had spoken just before the argument erupted.

"I never found anyone I wanted to spend the rest of my life with, the way I'd hoped to do with you."

Thirteen

Dressed in a leopard-print gown and peignoir set, Olivia poured herself another bourbon on the rocks and sipped it slowly as she went to stand by the window of her Sutton Place apartment high above New York City.

Her conversation with Pete Mulligan two nights ago was keeping her awake, and what was left of the ten thousand dollars he had given her was burning a hole in her pocket. She had already lost two thousand dollars at the roulette table and was afraid to try to win back the money for fear she'd lose it all.

Yet, she had to do something. The contractor had already called her twice at work, demanding to know why she wasn't returning his calls. If she kept stalling, he'd start demanding his money back.

What the hell was she going to do then?

The phone rang, causing her to almost drop her glass. She threw a nervous glance at the clock. Eleven-fifteen. Who would call at this time of night? It couldn't be Mulligan. She hadn't given him her home phone number.

Suddenly worried something may have happened to her mother, she yanked the phone from the cradle. "Hello?"

"Hi, Olivia."

Her throat went dry as she recognized Mulligan's voice. "How did you get this number?"

"I have connections, babe. You ought to know that by now."

Not a man to waste time in formalities, he came straight to the point. "Where do we stand with those bids?"

Olivia swallowed. "Look, Pete, I…"

"You know I can't afford to wait much longer. The bids have to be in by December 20. I need time to write the damn thing."

"I can't do it—"

"You can't do it?"

"Don't be angry—"

"What the fuck do you mean, 'Don't be angry'? We had a deal. You took my money."

"I'll pay it back, Pete, I swear."

His voice turned thin and nasty. "You don't get it, do you, Olivia? I don't give a shit about the money. I want those bids."

"I know, but I…can't do it. I can't do that to my father. He—"

Mulligan hung up.

Despite a full schedule, Philip Van Horn had agreed to meet Dan for a quick lunch at a nearby pub. As Dan, who sat at the bar, saw the attorney cut through the heavy crowd, he stood up.

"Thanks for meeting me, Philip," he said, shaking his hand. "Especially on such short notice."

"No problem." Philip took the stool next to him.

"It's good to see you again, Dan. It's been a while, hasn't it?"

"Twelve years." Dan waited until both had ordered BLTs and iced tea, before adding, "I'm sorry about Blair, Philip. I had no idea until Jill told me."

Van Horn pressed his lips together in what may have been an attempt to smile. "Thank you."

Sensing he didn't want to discuss his daughter's death, Dan quickly came to the point. "I take it Jill told you why I wanted to talk to you."

Philip nodded. "She said you were investigating Simon's death and were trying to find out who may have had a reason to kill him."

"That pretty much sums it up. She gave me a list of people her father knew—friends, clients, acquaintances—and I'm checking each one of them out, but that's going to take a while. That's why I appreciate your seeing me, Philip. You might help me expedite things a little."

"I'm not sure I can help you but I'll try."

"You and Simon knew the same people. You also worked with him, even socialized with him. If someone hated him enough to kill him, you'd know, wouldn't you?"

"Possibly. But to tell you the truth, Dan, I'm having a hard time accepting the idea Simon was murdered. He was a good man, brilliant at his job, thoughtful and generous to a fault. The idea that someone would want to kill him sounds—and I don't mean to insult you or Jill—ridiculous."

Dan studied the man's face closely but saw nothing other than genuine concern. "If my memory is correct,

he could also be hot-tempered and sometimes unfor-
giving.''

Philip smiled. ''Aren't we all? To some extent?''

''I suppose so.'' Dan watched the bartender set their
plates down. ''At the moment, however, I'm interested
in only one man—Simon—and whether his temper
ever got him in trouble.''

''Not to my knowledge. The staff thought very
highly of him. So did our clients. If he blew up once
in a while, they forgave him.''

Dan took a healthy bite of his BLT. After he'd swallowed the mouthful, he continued, ''And in all the
years you've known Simon, you've never witnessed
anything unusual? Anything that gave you pause?''

For the first time since Dan had begun the questioning, Philip looked ill at ease. Picking up his sandwich, he stared at it for a moment. ''Maybe we should
end our conversation right here,'' he said. ''I just don't
feel comfortable discussing this with you.''

Dan sat up straight. ''So there *is* something you're
not telling me.''

''I didn't say that.''

''Come on, you might as well have.'' When Philip
didn't answer, Dan leaned forward in his stool.
''Philip, listen to me. A man you and I cared about a
lot is dead and now the same thing could happen to
Jill.''

Philip looked mildly alarmed. ''What are you talking about? Did someone threaten her?''

''No,'' Dan said, bound by his promise not to tell
anyone about the attack on Jill the other night. ''But
I have reason to believe Jill could be in danger, so if
there is anything you can tell me that will help me

protect her better, or help me catch a killer, please tell me.''

A heavy silence fell between the two men, but Dan made no effort to break it. Van Horn was an attorney. He knew the implications of holding back evidence as well as Dan did. "Well, Counselor?" Dan asked.

Philip put his untouched sandwich back on his plate. Resting his elbows on the bar top, he ran his hands down his face, his expression weary. "Simon was having an affair."

Dan gave him a startled look. *"An affair?"*

"I know. I had difficulty believing it myself at first."

"Did he confide in you?"

"No. I found out by accident. It was toward the end of September, I believe. Simon and I were working late when the woman's husband burst into Simon's office and began to scream obscenities at him. Thank God everyone had already gone home."

"Who was the man?"

"Pete Mulligan. Simon was having an affair with his wife, Vivian."

Dan leaned back in his stool. "Well, I'll be damned."

"The argument started to get out of hand. I had to step in and stop them from killing each other. They had a long history of mutual hatred. A few months earlier, Mulligan had accused Simon of rigging bids, which of course wasn't true."

"Did Mulligan threaten Simon?"

"On that second visit he did. He told him he was going to kill him. He might have, too, if I hadn't threatened to call the police."

"And Simon didn't report the incident?"

"How could he? He knew that if he filed a complaint, he'd have to expose his affair with Vivian. That's why he applied for a gun permit, to protect himself from Mulligan. I guess after a few days, he forgot about it and never pursued it."

Philip drank his iced tea. "When I heard that Jill had found the permit application, I had to pretend I didn't know anything about it. I felt lousy lying to her, but I couldn't tell her. I had given Simon my word that his secret was safe with me."

And from what Dan knew about the attorney, his word was as binding as an ironclad contract. "I take it Mulligan didn't say anything, either."

"I'm sure he would have if it hadn't been for his wife's job. She teaches fifth-grade English at a very exclusive private girls' school. The trustees would have never tolerated such behavior on the part of one of their teachers."

So if Mulligan was hell-bent on revenge, Dan mused, his only other recourse would have been murder. But why kill Simon two months after that violent argument instead of right away, while the rage was still hot?

Dan took a long, deep breath. Simon an adulterer. He still couldn't believe it. He had seen Jill's father with Amanda. He had seen the way he talked to her, smiled at her, whispered in her ear at times, like a lover sharing a secret. No man could have loved his wife more, or been more proud of her.

And of all the women he could have had, he had gone after Mulligan's wife.

Had he tried to get back at him for those accusations a few months earlier? Or had he been just plain stupid?

It was one forty-five when Jill's secretary buzzed her on the intercom. "Guess who's on line three?" she asked.

Jill smiled. Like Cecilia, Cathie had always been very fond of Dan and the news of his visit to New York, which she chose to regard as his "return" to New York, had been the subject of many discussions between her and the other secretaries.

"Only one man besides your husband could make you sound so lustful," Jill teased. "Dan Santini."

Cathie giggled. "Just don't tell Freddy. Shall I put Dan through?"

"Oh, why not?" Still annoyed at herself for losing her cool last night, Jill picked up the receiver. "I have tons of work, Dan, so make it quick."

Dan's voice was soft enough to make her skin tingle. "Quick was never my style, Red, you know that."

"Cut it out."

"Ouch."

She pressed a fist against her mouth to stifle a laugh. "I really *am* busy, Dan. What do you want?"

"To apologize about last night, for one thing. I was a jerk."

Though she blamed herself equally, she refused to admit it to him. "I won't disagree with you on that point. And I do accept your apologies. Was there anything else?"

"I found out something you need to hear."

Jill put her pen down. "Why don't I like the sound of that?"

"Can you take a break and meet me somewhere? I'd rather not discuss this at B&A."

"Not right now. I have to meet a client at a construction site in thirty-five minutes."

"How long will you be?"

"A couple of hours at the most."

"Then why don't we meet when you're finished? You pick the place."

She thought for a moment. "All right. The American Festival Café, at Rockefeller Plaza. At three?"

"I'll be there."

Fourteen

Eastside Academy was nestled between two elegant town houses and occupied all three floors of a restored prewar brownstone on Sixty-second Street.

The halls were dark and quiet when Dan arrived at two-fifteen. Seated at an antique rosewood desk in the small lobby, an attractive receptionist gave Dan a quick, appraising glance.

"Can I help you?" she asked pleasantly.

"I hope so. My name is Dan Santini. I'm here to see Mrs. Mulligan."

"Do you have an appointment?"

"I'm afraid not."

"Are you a parent?"

Dan shook his head.

The young woman's smile was apologetic. "I'm sorry, Mr. Santini. Our teachers don't see anyone without an appointment. I'll be glad to arrange—"

"I think she'll see me," Dan said easily. "Tell her we have a mutual friend by the name of Simon."

After a short hesitation, the young woman pushed her chair back and stood up. "She might be in class right now, but I'll check."

Less than a minute later she was back. She was smiling again. "You may go in, Mr. Santini." She pointed to a door at the end of the corridor. "Third office on your right."

Dan's first thought when he saw Vivian Mulligan was that he couldn't blame Simon. In her late thirties, she had pale blond hair held back with a black scarf, arresting brown eyes and a wide, sexy mouth that didn't quite match the prim image she was trying to convey. Even the severe gray suit, accented with a black silk blouse, wasn't able to totally transform her into a schoolmarm.

From the pallor of her cheeks, Dan suspected she was either in poor health or his mention of Simon's name had had the desired effect. He bet on the latter.

"Mr. Santini." Walking back to her desk, she pointed to a chair. "I don't believe we've met."

"We haven't," Dan said. "But it was kind of you to fit me in." Dan sat down.

She didn't return his smile. "I have to meet the mother of one of my students at two forty-five, Mr. Santini, so please let's not play games, shall we? Who are you and what do you want?"

He had to admire her directness and the unflinching way she held his gaze. He was also grateful for it. It made his job infinitely easier. "I'm investigating Simon Bennett's death."

She blinked. "I thought his death was ruled accidental."

"It was, but there may be reason to believe otherwise."

A long, elegant hand went up to smooth down her hair, which didn't need smoothing. "What does that have to do with me?"

"You were a friend of Simon's, weren't you? An *intimate* friend."

"Who told you that?"

"That's not important, Mrs. Mulligan. What is important is that your affair with Simon could put you and your husband in a rather compromising situation."

Her complexion paled even more, but other than that, she gave no sign of discomfort. "You're not a police detective or you would have already shown me your badge, so what exactly *is* your capacity in this matter, Mr. Santini? Are you an attorney? A private investigator?"

"Neither. I'm a former homicide detective for NYPD. I occasionally act as a consultant for various police departments throughout the country."

"Are you acting as a consultant now?"

The woman was even sharper than he had realized. "No, I'm not."

"Then I don't have to talk to you, do I?"

"Is that what you choose to do?"

She was thoughtful for a moment, as if considering her answer. After a while, she folded her arms and rested them on her desk. "What exactly do you want to know?"

"Were you romantically involved with Simon Bennett?"

She looked at him for a good five seconds before answering. "Yes. He and I met at a charity function last year."

"And your husband found out?"

"He didn't find out. I told him. I couldn't bear the deception anymore."

"I see. How did he take it?"

Her smile was mildly condescending. "How would *you* take it, Mr. Santini?"

This time it was his turn not to return the smile. "I don't know, Mrs. Mulligan. I've never had anyone cheat on me before."

She didn't even blink. "You wouldn't like it. Any more than Pete did. He flew into a rage. He even went to confront Simon, which you already know or you wouldn't be here."

Some of her earlier tension was gone, as if admitting the affair had taken a great weight off her shoulders. "But if you think Pete killed him..." She shook her head. "You couldn't be more wrong."

"There's a witness who says your husband threatened to kill him."

"And that's all he did. Ask anyone in this city and they'll tell you that one of my husband's greatest pleasures is to push people around and frighten them. They'll also tell you that he's quick to back down when he meets his match. Simon was a formidable opponent, Mr. Santini, and Pete knew it. As for committing murder." She shook her head again. "I'm sure he may have been tempted, but he wouldn't do it. My husband doesn't have the killer instinct. He's all bark and no bite."

Dan leaned back in his chair and watched her intently. "What about you, Mrs. Mulligan? Do you have the killer instinct?"

She regarded him calmly. "I might have, under certain circumstances, but I didn't kill Simon, if that's your question. I had no reason to."

"Were the two of you still involved when he died?"

"No. The affair was over. I broke it off."

"When was that?"

"In late September. The same day I told Pete."

"Just to satisfy my curiosity, where were you on the night of December 1?"

She must have been prepared for the question because she answered it without the slightest hesitation. "My husband and I went to bed at the same time—shortly after ten."

"Both of you stayed there until morning?"

"I certainly did, and I have no reason to believe Pete wasn't there with me. I'm a very light sleeper, Mr. Santini. If my husband had slipped out of bed at any time during the night, I would have heard him."

As Dan stood up to leave, Vivian Mulligan stood up with him. Her cool, businesslike demeanor softened. "I have taught here at Eastside Academy since I graduated from college sixteen years ago," she said. "If it were to be known that I..." For the first time since Dan had entered her office, that remarkable poise he'd admired so much seemed to falter.

He experienced a quick feeling of compassion for her. It was obvious that, despite her involvement with Simon, Vivian Mulligan loved her husband. And she valued her job at Eastside Academy immensely.

"I hope it doesn't come to that, Mrs. Mulligan," he replied in answer to her half-spoken plea. "I wish I could be more reassuring, but right now that's the best I can do."

He could tell it wasn't the answer she wanted to hear, but she accepted it, with a slight nod of her head. "I understand."

Outside Eastside Academy, Dan looked at the row of black limousines that were already lining up along the curb, ready to pick up the school's well-to-do students, then back at the elegant building he had just left. This was one of Manhattan's most elite private schools, an establishment of such fame and prestige that enrollment began at birth and yearly tuition set parents back a whopping forty grand a year. Yet there was nothing within those tony walls that he would want for his children, not the education, not the social status and certainly not the morality.

Glancing at his watch, he saw that it was almost two-thirty. Enough time to get the Land Rover out of the parking garage and drive to Rockefeller Center to meet Jill.

Raising the collar of his leather jacket, Dan jammed his hands in his pockets and headed toward the parking sign at the end of the street.

The American Festival Café, on the lower level of Rockefeller Plaza was filled with its usual crowd of students, tourists and office workers when Jill arrived a little after three.

Outside on the ice rink, skaters with varying degrees of expertise, glided and whirled to the tune of "Silent Night." Just behind the golden statue of Prometheus, a seventy-five-foot Norway spruce, the city's most famous *tannenbaum*, rose gloriously above it all, thousands of bright Christmas lights strung through it.

The Festival Café looked equally festive, with a tree of its own at the restaurant's entrance and small, red poinsettias dotting every table.

Jill stood just inside the door and scanned the crowded room. Spotting Dan at a window booth in the back, she indicated to the hostess where she was going and wove her way through the tables.

"Hi." Dan stood up. "You look great."

As always, the unexpected compliment seemed to take her by surprise, a reaction that never ceased to amaze him. "Thank you." She turned to the hostess who was holding a menu. "Just coffee for me, please, black."

Dan watched her shrug off her red wool coat. Underneath she wore a simple black pants suit with a whimsical pin in the shape of a grinning alligator on the lapel. With all the expensive jewelry her parents had given her over the years, she had always preferred the versatility of simpler, inexpensive pieces, little trinkets that caught her fancy and matched her mood of the moment.

"Everything okay with that job you had to look at?"

"Yes, thank God. For a minute, I thought we were going to lose another client, but we didn't, so I suppose I can relax. Until next time."

"Has it been that bad without Simon?"

"Worse than I could have imagined. I loved and admired my father very much, and to a certain extent I understand our clients' reaction, but they make me so mad. Do they really believe that B&A is what it is today because of just one man? Don't they read our brochures, keep up with our architects' achievements? See the great buildings they have designed? The awards they've won?"

Dan was mildly surprised. This passion for her job, this pride in her own people, was a side of her he didn't know. But he liked it very much. "I'm sure you set them straight."

She fought a smile. "Well…in a gentle, diplomatic way." When the waiter had brought her coffee, she picked up her cup but didn't drink from it right away. "So, what's the bad news?"

Dan stirred a teaspoonful of sugar into his coffee. Earlier he had debated whether or not to tell Jill about Simon's affair. She had worshiped the man, and he hated to be the one to rock that faith. But what choice did he have? Their newly founded partnership, no matter how temporary, was based on one simple factor—total honesty. And if he wanted Jill to trust him, he would have to abide by the rules.

Her stare was almost painful. "Come on, Dan."

"I found out your father was having an affair."

Jill's shoulders stiffened. "Who told you that?"

"Philip Van Horn."

"Philip?"

He could read her like a book, see everything that was going through her head. She was shocked and outraged that one of the people she trusted the most was spreading such ugly rumors about her father. "Philip didn't make it up," he said, anxious to restore her faith in the attorney. "He didn't even want to tell me. The only reason he did was because I didn't give him much of a choice."

Jill had turned livid. "Why are you siding with him? What did he do to make you believe such a lie?"

"He didn't do anything. Philip was in your father's office the night the woman's husband barged in and accused him of sleeping with his wife. And your father didn't deny it. The two men almost killed each other,

Jill. God knows what would have happened if Philip hadn't been there.''

Her anger quickly fading, she raised stricken eyes at him. ''It's not true. My father would never do anything like that. He loved my mother.'' Then, as he remained silent, she asked, ''Who's the woman?''

He hesitated for only a few seconds. ''Vivian Mulligan.''

This time she stared at him, stone-still. ''That's ridiculous. My father hated Mulligan.''

''Apparently the feeling didn't extend to his wife.''

Her lips set in a tight line, Jill turned to look out the window. A young girl in red leggings and a Santa's hat was doing double axels drawing cheers from the crowd. But Jill's festive mood had vanished. She felt betrayed, which, of course, was a stupid, childish reaction. This wasn't about *her*. It was about her father. And why was she so shocked, anyway? Hadn't she already suspected that another woman was involved? Wasn't that the reason she had gone to Washington?

''How long...were they together?''

''A few months. Apparently Vivian broke up with your father the day she told her husband about the affair.''

Jill pressed her fingers to her temples where a headache was beginning to throb. Her father had carried on an affair right here in New York City and no one *knew?* How could that be? When had he turned into such a skillful deceiver?

''Are you okay?''

Dan's concerned voice brought her back. ''No. If you want to know the truth, I feel pretty damn rotten right now.''

Dan's hand closed on hers. "Simon's affair had nothing to do with you, Jill, or his love for you."

She yanked her hand away. "You're defending him! What a typical male reaction."

"I'm not defending him."

"How could he do something so awful?"

"Parents don't always come in perfect, flawless packages. They're human, too."

Challenging blue eyes held his, the way they had so many times before. "Would your father have cheated on Angelina?"

"No."

"Would you have cheated on me?"

"Never."

"Then how can you speak of adultery as if it was something men do because...they're men."

"That's not what I'm doing. And I'm certainly not condoning what your father did. I just don't want to see you destroyed by something that was beyond your control."

He was right. Sitting here and brooding wasn't going to accomplish anything. Her father's actions angered her but deep down, she knew they wouldn't affect her love for him, or her determination to find his killer.

"I, too, have something to tell you." She kept her eyes downcast. "Something I should have told you earlier, but didn't."

She half expected him to make some sort of sarcastic remark. Instead he folded his hands on the table and said quietly, "I'm listening."

"A few days ago, I found out my father had taken a trip to Washington, D.C., on October 3, a time when he should have been in Miami attending a very important business meeting.'' Because her hands had suddenly grown cold, she wrapped them around her coffee cup to warm them. "No one seemed to know anything about that trip—not my mother, not Henry, who had taken my dad to the airport, and not even Cecilia. To make matters even more mysterious, Carl Jenner, the man whom Daddy should have met in Miami, said that my father called him the day before to say he wouldn't be attending the meeting after all. An emergency had come up.

"I should have told you the other night when we agreed to be truthful with each other, but I couldn't.'' She lowered her head. "I was afraid there might be another woman involved and I was embarrassed.''

"It's okay, Jill. I understand. Do you know what that emergency was?''

Jill shook her head. "No one seems to know that, either.'' She forced herself to look up, to meet his gaze. "I went to Washington on Monday, hoping to get some answers, but I struck out.''

Dan's gaze sharpened. "I thought you went to Richmond.''

"I did. I just made sure to get a return flight with a long enough layover in Washington to allow me time to make a few inquiries.''

"That could have been dangerous, Jill.''

"But it wasn't. And I was able to talk to a skycap by the name of Tyrone. He remembers my father taking a cab for destination unknown, but can't remember the name of the cab company. He's agreed to keep an eye out for the driver.''

The worried crease between Dan's brows was slowly disappearing. "Did you talk to anyone else?"

"Three cab companies. No luck there, either, but they said they'd call if they located the driver." She took a sip of her cold coffee. "The mystery may be solved, anyway," she said bitterly. "The destination was probably some romantic hideaway, and the woman he met there was Vivian Mulligan."

"I don't think so. According to Vivian, the affair was over by then."

"Have you talked to her?" Jill asked, surprised.

"Yes. I just came from meeting with her."

"She could have lied."

"Why would she? What difference would it make to her when they broke up?"

Jill lifted a stubborn chin. "It would direct the suspicion to her, that's the difference it would make."

Dan felt the new anger and understood it. Having learned the identity of her father's mistress, she was now focusing all her rage on that one person. It was a normal reaction, one that would eventually run its course.

"I'll check out every possibility," he said gently. "I promise."

Appearing to be soothed, she looked at him. "How will you do that? You don't have the resources you once had as an NYPD detective."

He smiled, glad that all that resentment hadn't dulled her thought processes. "I still have a few connections here and there. And I've hired a private detective."

"You've what?"

An elderly couple at the next table glanced in their

direction, obviously straining to hear more. Dan leaned across the table and spoke in a low, hushed voice. "Relax, Jill. I've known Al Metzer for a long time. He's competent, trustworthy and, above all, discreet."

"I don't want him questioning my family. My mother would never stand for it, or my uncle."

"He won't. He's helping me check out a few people, that's all. Right now he's looking into Mulligan's background. I expect to hear from him at any moment." Glancing at the couple across the aisle, he took her hand and squeezed it. "Trust me, okay?"

Trusting him was the easy part, Jill thought as she looked down at their joined hands. Even in their darkest moments, she had always been able to count on him, though not always in ways she expected.

What would their life be like, she wondered, if they had stayed married? Would they have children? Would they be feverishly preparing for the holidays right now, hurrying up and down Manhattan in search of the latest toys? Hiding presents under the bed?

She had a sudden vision of Dan hoisting a toddler onto his shoulders as the Macy's Christmas parade went by. What a great father he would have made, and how strange that he, who loved children so much, had never remarried and started a family of his own.

"You're doing it again."

She looked up to find him smiling. "Doing what?"

"Drifting out on me."

There was a question in his eyes, but she had a feeling he already knew what she had been thinking. And that worried her almost as much as those crazy thoughts she'd been having lately. "It's nothing important." She gathered her coat around her shoulders and slid across the banquette, dragging her purse behind her. "Call me as soon as you know something, okay? Right now I have to get to the office and finish a couple of things."

"I'll give you a ride back."

Dan dropped a few bills on the table and followed her out. The holiday season was putting him in a strange mood, and judging from the look on Jill's face a moment ago, it was doing the same to her.

As they walked to the garage on Fifty-first Street, an item in a store window they passed caught his eye. He glanced at it only briefly, but in a split second his mind had registered every detail.

Jill abruptly turned to look at him. "What's going on? Who are you smiling at?"

He chuckled. "Nothing. I thought I saw someone I knew."

The watch on Jill's wrist read six-thirty when the phone on her desk rang. Knowing Cathie had already gone home, she picked it up on the first ring.

"Miz Bennett," a low baritone drawled. "This here's Tyrone."

Jill felt a leap of excitement. "Tyrone. Did you find out something?"

"Sure did. The cab your father took that morning was here today. The driver remembers your father and where he took him, because it was kind of an unusual place for a man to go to."

Jill's grip on the receiver tightened. "Where was that, Tyrone?"

"A place called Alternatives, in Fairfax, Virginia," Tyrone replied. "An abortion clinic."

Fifteen

The receiver still pressed to her ear, Jill slowly sat down. "Abortion clinic?"

"That's what the man said."

Her head swam as she tried to comprehend what she had just heard. "Did the cab wait for my father?"

"Nope. Just dropped him off and drove away."

"Thank you, Tyrone. I'll make sure you and your friend get that money I promised you right away. Where should I send it?"

On a pad that lay on her desk, she wrote down the address as well as the address of Alternatives, thanked him again and hung up.

An abortion clinic. With each passing second the words seemed to grow more ominous. She could come up with only one explanation why her father had gone to such a place. He had made someone pregnant— unless the cabdriver had made a mistake, which was entirely possible. After all, it was more than two months since he'd picked up that fare. How many faces had he seen since then? Hundreds?

Picking up the phone again, she dialed her travel agent and booked a flight to Washington, D.C., for the following morning. Then she called Cathie's answering machine, leaving a message that she had to go out of town and would be back at three the following afternoon. When she was finished, she called Dan, whom she knew would be helping his mother close the shop, and told him what she had just found out.

"I'll come with you," he offered.

"No, Dan, that's not necessary. I'm only going there and back. There's absolutely no danger. I'll call you when I get home."

Before he could argue, she hung up.

As Dan slowly put the receiver back in the cradle, Angelina, who was busy scrubbing the already immaculate counters in the back storeroom, looked at him. "Was that Jill?"

"Yes."

"You look worried, Danny. What is it?"

He tried to brush her concern aside. "Nothing."

"Don't give me that. I could hear the worry in your voice just now. And I overheard you and your brother talking last night after dinner. Why didn't you tell me you were investigating Simon's death?"

"I didn't want to worry you. And I wasn't entirely sure there was something to investigate."

"And now you are?"

Rather than answer the question, he braced his shoulder against the doorjamb and folded his arms across his chest. "Can I ask you something?"

She started to put the utensils she had used during the day in their respective places. "Of course, you can."

"What did you think of Simon, Ma? I mean, did you like him?"

If she thought the question strange, she didn't show

it. "Yes, I liked him. It was hard not to. He was always in a good mood, he joked around and he never treated me or your father as anything but his equals." She looked up in the distance for a moment before returning to her task.

Because Dan knew that his mother's intuition was almost as keen as his own, his curiosity was instantly aroused. "What is it, Ma?"

"I'm not sure. I don't quite know how to put it." She dropped a handful of clean silverware into a drawer. "At times I felt sorry for him."

"Sorry for Simon?" Dan had never thought of his ex-father-in-law as a man who inspired pity. "Why?"

"I always had the feeling he wasn't completely happy, that something was missing from his life."

"Did he ever say anything to make you feel that way?"

"Not exactly, but he always seemed to be talking about the things he hadn't done yet rather than what he had already accomplished. He was always afraid there wouldn't be enough time to do it all, that he was growing old too fast."

"Lots of men fear old age, Ma."

"Not like Simon." She untied her apron and tossed it in a hamper. "One time, he told your father and me that having young people around him made him feel vital, strong, capable of doing anything. That's when I started feeling sorry for him. He had everything a man could want, a lovely family, a successful business, fame, wealth, and all he wanted was to be young again." She shook her head as if the logic of that thought escaped her.

Worried about getting old. That was another side of

Simon he hadn't known about. Could that fear be the reason he'd had an affair with a woman twenty-five years his junior? Dan gave a mental shrug. It was an interesting facet of Simon's character, but hardly a solution to his murder.

Unless, Dan mused, Amanda had found out about the affair and in a moment of rage had killed her husband. It was a wild idea, but considering he also suspected Vivian Mulligan, it was just as conceivable for a jealous wife to have killed her cheating husband as it was for a mistress to do the same. Maybe more so.

"Why did you want to know what I thought of Simon?" Angelina asked.

"He was a complex man. And you're a sensible woman. Your thoughts gave me a new insight on him, and that's always helpful."

"Good. Now maybe you can do something for me."

"Uh-oh."

"All I want is for you to bring Jill over for dinner. I know she'll probably want to spend a quiet Christmas at home with her mother this year, but what about this Sunday? We'd all love to see her and I'm sure the boys would enjoy meeting her."

"She won't come, Ma."

"How do you know? You haven't asked her yet." She took a quilted gray jacket from a hook on the wall and slipped it on. "I think being around happy, noisy, well-adjusted people is just what the girl needs to lift her spirits."

She was probably right, Dan thought. Sunday dinners at the Santinis used to be a ritual when he and Jill were married. An only child, Jill had loved the warm atmosphere, the laughter and the loud, heated discussions as they passed the homemade pasta around the table.

Looking back, he couldn't remember a time when his young bride had looked happier. "All right, Ma. I'll ask her."

As predicted by the TV weatherman, snow had begun to fall over northern Virginia a little after midnight, just as Cynthia Parson was finishing her shift at Alternatives, the abortion clinic where she had worked for the past seven years.

Now, as she drove home at the end of her four-to-midnight shift, the snow intensified, making visibility more difficult. Flipping her windshield wipers to high, she leaned forward, her eyes narrowing as she concentrated on the dark road ahead. She hated to drive at night, and liked it even less in bad weather.

When the Conti Farms sign came into view, she sighed with relief. Her turnoff was just beyond that. She wouldn't be late after all and Vera wouldn't have to worry about her.

God bless the woman, Cynthia thought as she slowed down to negotiate the turn. Not only did she take care of Molly as if she were her own daughter, she fussed over Cynthia as well, always worrying about her, getting dinner started, dispensing advice, just as Cynthia's mother used to do.

Until she found Vera, Cynthia had never imagined entrusting her precious little girl to anyone other than the girl's father. But when Collin, who had run his computer business from home, had died so suddenly a year ago last Thanksgiving, she'd had no choice but to find someone to help her with Molly.

Of all the baby-sitters Cynthia had interviewed for the job, only Vera had shown the patience, love and understanding needed to care for a child suffering from separation anxiety disorder.

Molly's illness had begun shortly after Collin's death. Terrified at the thought that Cynthia would die as well, the six-year-old had suddenly refused to go to school or leave her mother for any length of time. Every time Cynthia attempted to go to work, Molly would become so hysterical that the neighbors would come out in the street, wondering what Cynthia was doing to her child.

The therapist she had selected, though highly competent, had told Cynthia that for his sessions to be successful, he had to see Molly at least three times a week. But when the medical insurance for Molly had run out shortly after Thanksgiving, Cynthia hadn't been able to pay for the therapy on her own.

Even with the double shifts she volunteered for a couple of times a week, her salary barely covered her living expenses and the debts she and Collin had accumulated over the years.

And then two weeks ago, everything had changed.

The cell phone she always kept near her rang just as she turned onto Elbow Lane, cutting short her thoughts. Worried something might be wrong with Molly, she picked it up. "Hello?"

"Cynthia, it's Jack."

Cynthia's heart did a somersault. The man she knew as Jack Smith was the last person she had expected to hear from this evening. As far as she knew, her obligations to him had been fulfilled, and if she never saw or heard from him again, that would be just fine with her.

"Cynthia, are you there?"

"Yes." She cleared her throat. "Is something wrong?"

"You could say that."

Cynthia groaned.

"Relax, it's only a mild setback, nothing you can't handle."

"Why don't you let me be the judge of that?" Half a block from the cul-de-sac where she lived, she stopped her Ford wagon and turned off the lights. If she went any closer to her house, Vera might see her through the window. "What happened?" she asked. "Did someone find out about me?"

"Not you specifically, just the clinic, and that Simon Bennett was there on October 3."

"Oh, God." Something icy settled in the pit of her stomach. "Who is it? The police?"

"Simon's daughter. Her name is Jill Bennett."

"Great."

"Listen to me. When she comes to see you tomorrow morning, all you have to do is deny that Simon Bennett was ever there. And don't give her any of that doctor-patient privilege crap—it'll only make her more suspicious. Tell her you've never seen the man or heard the name."

He made it sound so easy. He wasn't the one who had to live with the lie and the fear every day. He wasn't the one they would be questioning. "What makes you think she'll believe me? If she's got that far, she can't be stupid."

"Far from it. But all she knows is that her father came to the clinic. Be convincing when you tell her he didn't and she'll leave thinking whoever gave her the information made a mistake." He paused. "I'm a little worried about your boss, though. What do you think he'll do if she questions him?"

"You don't have to worry about Dr. Laken. He's a fanatic about that doctor-patient privilege information you have so little regard for." She couldn't help the dig. "His entire reputation depends not only on his skills but also on his discretion. Without it, he might as well close the clinic. No one would ever trust him again."

"Good."

Cynthia's hands tightened around the steering wheel. "I don't know if I can do this. Be questioned, I mean. It wasn't part of the deal."

"Pull yourself together," he said sharply. "You don't want to screw up now. You know what will happen if you do."

She closed her eyes. How could she forget? He must have told her a half-dozen times already. She would be arrested for withholding evidence, interrogated, maybe even put in jail. Even if the law spared her, Dr. Laken would not.

She didn't want to think about what would become of Molly if she no longer had a job.

"Cynthia, did you hear me?"

"I heard you." Tears of hopelessness stung her eyes as she glanced down the street. Only her modest Cape Cod house at the end was still lit up. In the middle of the lawn, a huge Santa and his sleigh stood facing the street.

"And you'll do what you have to?"

Suddenly she wanted out of this car, out of this man's reach. She wanted to be inside her safe little house, with her precious little daughter. "Yes, I'll do what I have to."

"Good girl." There was another short pause. "How's Molly?"

She shivered. There it was again, that veiled threat. He did that so well. It could almost pass for fatherly concern. Cynthia knew better. It was his way of telling her he knew everything about her, just as he had known which of the three nurses at the clinic to approach, which one would be the most vulnerable.

"Molly's fine," she said at last. "Now, if that's all, I'd like to go home."

"Watch out for Jill Bennett," he warned. "She's a bright young woman. And she's intuitive as hell when it comes to people."

"I thought you said I had nothing to worry about."

"You don't, as long as you don't panic."

The click at the other end told her he had hung up. She did the same and dropped the cell phone into her purse. Trembling, Cynthia sat in the dark car, wishing she had never heard of this horrible man. Night after night, she lay awake, thinking about what she had done, wishing she could turn back the clock and change everything.

She knew nothing about him other than what he had told her. By the time she realized that he had killed a man, she was too deeply involved to do anything about it. She had already used some of the money to pay off her debts as well as Molly's therapy sessions. The rest of the fifty thousand dollars had been placed in a safe-deposit box so no one would find out about it.

It had all seemed so innocent at first. A man had shown up on her doorstep and introduced himself as Jack Smith. In a voice that was remarkably steady for a man she assumed was in his late sixties, he told her that he suspected his wife of having had an abortion and needed Cynthia's help in identifying the man who had come with her to Alternatives.

When Cynthia had refused to answer his questions, he had offered to give her fifty thousand dollars for her trouble.

"You'll finally be able to help your little girl," he had told her. "Give her the medical care she so desperately needs."

That should have been her first clue right there. What kind of man could find out so much information about someone he'd never met?

Furious, she had slammed the door in his face.

But Jack was a persistent man. Two days later, he was back, and this time he had the money with him. In awe, because she had never seen so much cash at one time, Cynthia kept staring at it. It was enough money to put Molly back in therapy, and Cynthia could stop working all those late shifts and spend more time with her little girl.

"Jack" had only wanted her to identify the two people in the picture he had brought with him. He'd even given her names, Julia Banks and Simon Bennett, so all she'd had to do was nod.

Aware that tears were streaming down her face, Cynthia quickly wiped them off. She couldn't let Vera know she had been crying. She'd want to know why.

After giving herself another minute, she put the car back in gear and drove the short distance to her house.

As usual, the nanny met her at the door with a cheery smile. She was a petite woman with kind blue eyes and short, tightly permed gray hair. "I was beginning to worry about you," she said. "I wasn't sure you had your snow tires on yet."

Cynthia hung her coat in the closet and tried not to think of Jill Bennett's visit tomorrow morning. "I had them installed last week. Just in time, it seems."

Lifting the edge of the dark blue drapes, Vera glanced outside. "It's snowing quite hard, isn't it?"

"Too hard for you to venture out at this time of night," Cynthia replied. "Why don't you stay here tonight, Vera?"

Vera accepted without hesitation. A widow with no one at home waiting for her, she always kept a change of clothes in the spare bedroom in case of such emergencies.

With an exhausted sigh, Cynthia sank into a big overstuffed chair and removed her white oxfords. Reaching down, she rubbed her tired feet. "How was Molly today?"

"Quiet. She seemed a little tired so I put her to bed early."

Cynthia rose from the chair, and in her white-stocking feet, walked down the carpeted hallway and into her daughter's room. The clown night-light cast a soft golden glow on the sleeping child. Silky blond hair framed her rounded cheeks, and her small, heart-shaped mouth was slightly open. Tightly clutched in her arms was Charlotte, her favorite doll.

A lump formed in Cynthia's throat. In the seven

short years she had performed the nightly ritual, this emotional reaction at the sight of her daughter had never varied.

Bending over the bed, she pressed her lips against the child's smooth forehead, said a silent good-night to her and quietly tiptoed away.

A moment before, she had been terrified at the thought of meeting Jill Bennett face-to-face in the morning. But seeing Molly lying here, looking so peaceful, and knowing she would be getting better soon, instilled her with new strength.

She would be all right. She had to be.

Sixteen

After a quick dinner that had consisted of a cheese sandwich and a can of Campbell's cream of mushroom soup, Jill put the dirty dishes into the dishwasher and wondered why she even bothered. Most of the time she had to wait almost a week, until she had a full load, before turning the machine on.

One of these days, she'd learned how to cook and put all those fancy appliances to good use.

She was considering taking the dishes out and washing them by hand when the bell rang, not once but several times in rapid succession.

"All right, all right." As she approached the door, she called out. "Is that you, Ashley?"

"No. It's Pete Mulligan."

She could hear the anger simmering in his voice. "What do you want?"

"I need to talk to you, dammit. Open the door, Jill, or I swear I'll—"

Before he could even finish his threat, Jill had flung the door open. "Or you'll do what, Mulligan? Break it down?"

Ignoring her, the contractor stormed in, looking as if he could take on an entire S.W.A.T. team with the sheer force of his fury.

"Who the fuck do you think you are?" he bellowed, his face inches from hers. "Sending that two-bit cop to question my wife." The tendons on his neck looked about ready to explode. "What right does he think he has anyway? He's not a detective anymore. And he sure as hell doesn't have anything on me."

Jill, too angry to be frightened, glared at him. "A private citizen doesn't need permission to question people. If your wife chose to talk to Dan, take it up with her instead of coming here and pushing your weight around. In case you haven't noticed, this isn't the Middle Ages anymore, so stop behaving like a caveman."

"I'll push my weight around all I want. I've had it with the Bennetts and their self-righteous attitude. You people are no better than the rest of us." He pointed a finger at her, his eyes mean and menacing. "And if that ex-husband of yours comes near my wife again, I'll file a harassment suit. Or better yet," he added, his lips pulling into a nasty sneer, "I'll come back and start harassing *you*. Maybe even teach you a lesson, see how he likes *that*."

"You come near her," a voice said from the doorway, "and I'll break you in half."

At the sound of Dan's voice, Jill spun around and almost flattened herself against the wall. She had never seen his eyes look like that—flat and cold—like those of a man capable of anything.

Before she could stop him, he had grabbed Mulligan by the lapels of his gray cashmere coat and backed him to the wall. "So unless you like pain, Mulligan, I suggest you hightail it out of here while you can still walk."

Mulligan's face turned beet red. "Take your fucking hands off of me, Santini, or—"

"Or you'll what?" Dan yanked him closer, almost lifting him off his feet.

But Mulligan, though hardly in a position to argue, kept his ground. "Or you'll be sorry. I have friends, you asshole. Friends who don't like it when jerks like you come snooping into my business, or try to pin a murder on me. Friends who jump when I say jump. You see where I'm going with this?"

Without loosening his grip, Dan glared at him. "Let's get a couple of things straight, Mulligan. First, you don't scare me. Second, as long as you remain a suspect, I'm going to be in your face whether you like it or not. Third, if I catch you within a hundred feet of Jill, here or at work, or anywhere on this planet, I'll break every bone in your body, one by one. Do you see where *I'm* going with this?"

Dan's rage must have struck a chord. Almost immediately, Mulligan's body relaxed. As Dan finally let him go, hard, the contractor staggered back and hit the little console in the entryway wall.

He didn't say a word, didn't even look back at Jill. After a while, he pulled his coat collar back in place, threw a murderous look at Dan and left.

One hand on her breast, Jill watched Dan slam the door shut. "I've never been so scared in my life. I thought you were going to kill him."

"I was tempted." His gaze narrowed on her face. "Are you all right? He didn't touch you, did he?"

"No."

He jammed a fist into his open hand. "I should have decked him, anyway. On principle."

Beginning to recover from the shock, Jill smiled. "I think the verbal assault was enough."

"You shouldn't have opened your door. What if he's the one who attacked you the other night?"

"If he is, he missed his big chance. He could have taken both of us down in one shot."

At the amused look in her eyes, Dan's anger began to recede. "What did he want?"

"He found out you'd questioned his wife. I guess he didn't like it." She motioned toward the living room. "Would you like a drink? Or a cup of coffee?" Because he hadn't fully let go of his fury yet, she added, "It's not every day that I get to repay a man for such chivalry."

He shook his head. "I don't want anything."

"All right." Puzzled, she looked at him. "Did you stop by for anything in particular? Or did that famous sixth sense of yours tell you I was in trouble?"

Looking suddenly awkward, he pulled a small square package from his pocket. It was wrapped in red foil and tied with a golden ribbon. "I know it isn't Christmas yet, but I saw this in a window earlier when we were walking, and…well, I know you like this kind of stuff."

Startled, she looked from him to the box. "You bought me a present?"

"You looked so sad when I told you about your father's affair, I thought you needed something to lift your spirits."

"Oh, Dan, I…"

He handed her the box. "Go ahead, open it."

She should have refused. Accepting his help without

even paying him for it was bad enough, but accepting a gift?

"Open it," he said again. "You can return it if you don't like it."

She was having difficulty keeping a straight face. A moment ago, he had looked dangerous enough, vicious enough to kill a man with his bare hands. And now he stood in front of her, anxious for her to open his gift and worried she wouldn't like it.

How could she possibly turn it down?

Without a word, she untied the ribbon and tore the pretty paper. Holding the box in one hand, she removed the lid and gasped. Nestled in black satin was an exquisite brooch made of gold filigree. The shape was that of a woman with gossamer wings attached to her sides. She was looking over her shoulder, with a mysterious smile on her lips and long, wavy hair cascading down her back.

"Oh, Dan, it's beautiful."

"You like it?"

"I love it. But it's…" She started to say "Much too expensive," but bit her tongue before the words came out.

As always, Dan had read her mind. "It's not an heirloom or anything, just something that caught my eye. And reminded me of you."

She looked up. "It did?"

"Uh-huh." Looking more relaxed now, he took the brooch and pinned it to her sweater. "Half siren, half angel. That's how I always thought of you."

"Really?"

"Really."

She looked down at the pin and let her fingers brush

against the delicate form. "And you came all the way from Brooklyn to give it to me."

"You know how I am when I buy a present."

She laughed. "Oh, I do. You're like a little kid." She kept her hand pressed against the pin. "Thank you, Dan. I'm really touched. And you were right. It does make me feel better."

"Good. Now, about tomorrow—"

She started to protest but he held a finger over her mouth. "I was only going to say to be careful. And to call me as soon as you get home."

"I'll do that."

She walked him to the door, waved as he stepped into the elevator, then closed the door.

He had always been, and probably would always be, the most generous, most thoughtful, most unpredictable man she knew.

How a woman hadn't already snatched him up was beyond her.

Seventeen

The wet snow that had greeted Jill at Washington National Airport when she'd arrived was still falling when her cab let her off at 1113 Old Mill Road in Fairfax.

Alternatives turned out to be an attractive two-story brick building overlooking a peaceful meadow and surrounded by tall and stately oaks. Traffic was practically nonexistent here, and from what the cabdriver had told her, the nearest commercial area was more than two miles away.

The receptionist lost her pleasant smile when she realized the kind of information Jill was after. "I'm sorry, Miss Bennett," she said pointedly. "The identity of our patients and the people who accompany them is kept strictly confidential."

"I'm aware of that," Jill said, "but this is terribly important."

Jill's polite plea had no effect on the woman.

"If you won't help me, then I'd like to talk to someone in charge," Jill said decisively. "The director of the clinic will do."

"That would be Dr. Ronald Laken, but I'm afraid he's in surgery at the moment."

"Does he have an assistant?"

The receptionist glanced at a chart on the wall. "His head nurse is on duty. She might be in the O.R. with him, however."

"Would you mind checking, please?"

Moments later, Jill heard her name being softly spoken. Looking up from the magazine she had been leafing through, she saw a trim young woman in a crisp white uniform. Not particularly pretty, she had short blond hair, a pert nose and sharp, intelligent eyes. On her left breast pocket a blue name tag identified her as Cynthia Parson, R.N.

"You wanted to see me?" she asked.

Jill stood up and introduced herself, but this time, rather than keep the reason for her visit vague, she told Cynthia Parson the truth, that her father had died under rather suspicious circumstances, and that she was trying to make some sense out of what she already knew.

Nurse Parson listened attentively, even compassionately. From time to time, she glanced at the picture Jill had handed her, but showed no sign of recognition. When Jill was finished, the young woman shook her head. "I'm sorry about your father, Miss Bennett. I wish I could help you, but..." She shook her head again.

"You don't remember him?"

"Not at all. And believe me, I would, if I had met him." She smiled and glanced at the photograph again before handing it back. "He's not someone a woman would easily forget."

This time, Jill didn't bother to conceal her disappointment. "I don't understand. A taxi brought him here, to this address."

"I don't know what to tell you."

"How can you be so sure he wasn't here?"

"Because I would have known. One of my duties here at Alternatives is to counsel every patient who comes in, before the doctor even sees them. If a husband, a boyfriend or a relative comes along, I talk to them as well, and make sure they know what to expect once the procedure is over."

"Were you on duty that day?"

"I work six days a week, so unless October 3 or 4 falls on a Sunday, I was here."

"Could you please check?"

"Of course." Walking over to the receptionist's desk, she spoke a few words, waited until she was handed a book and flipped through it quickly, then came back. "Both days fell on a weekday. Thursday and Friday, and I *was* on duty."

Jill felt as if her hopes of ever finding her father's killer were being shot down one by one. "Could my father have gone directly to Dr. Laken?" Jill asked. "Without you knowing about it?"

"I doubt it, but…" She hesitated. "I suppose that's possible."

"Then I'd like to talk to him, please. I know he's in surgery, but I'll wait."

Nurse Parson glanced at her watch. "Let me see how much longer he'll be," she said gently. "He may be able to talk to you for a few minutes."

"Thank you."

"Simon Bennett's daughter is in the waiting room. She found out her father was here on October 3 and she wants to talk to you."

In the room adjoining the O.R., Dr. Ronald Laken yanked off his rubber gloves and threw them in a special waste bin. He was a tall man with chiseled features and salt-and-pepper hair. "Dammit, Cynthia, why didn't you tell her I was busy?"

"Because she would have waited until you were free. She's a very determined young woman, Ron. Better talk to her."

"How did she find out her father was here?"

"Through the cabdriver who brought him to Alternatives."

"Damn."

Cynthia didn't echo his anxiety, though she was sure she felt it even more acutely than he did. Nor did she tell him about the man who had paid her fifty thousand dollars for information that should have remained confidential. Dr. Laken would have fired her on the spot if he knew.

Ron Laken and Simon Bennett had attended Harvard together, and when his old fraternity brother had turned to him for help, Ron had assured him that Simon's anonymity, as that of all the people who came to Alternatives, would be respected. Even now that Simon Bennett was dead, Ron Laken would not break that promise.

Within moments of their arrival, Simon Bennett's lady friend had been admitted under the name of Julia Banks, kept overnight, as a favor to Simon who was afraid of complications, and then discharged.

At the sink, Dr. Laken had just finished scrubbing his hands. "All right then," he said, taking the white towel Cynthia handed him. "If she's that stubborn, I guess I have no choice but to see Miss Bennett. I suppose the sooner I do that, the sooner she'll leave.''

Then, with a nod to Cynthia, he walked out of his office and went to meet Jill.

Standing in the rain outside the clinic, Jill flipped the hood of her London Fog over her head and looked helplessly around. Her lead had turned into nothing. A big fat zero. According to Dr. Laken, to whom she had talked for over ten minutes, her father had never set foot in the clinic. In fact, on October 3, Dr. Laken had performed only one abortion—on a nineteen-year-old girl who had brought her young husband with her. There were no other surgeries until the following Tuesday.

Jill had no reason to doubt him. Both he and Nurse Parson seemed like good, caring people who were genuinely concerned about her problem.

But if her father hadn't come to Alternatives, then where had he gone? There were no other office buildings on this road and several acres of bare land separated the clinic from the nearest shopping center.

Had he stopped here because he didn't want anyone to know where he was truly going? Had he proceeded on foot? Or had someone picked him up?

So many questions, she thought, peering down the road. And not a single answer that made sense.

For a moment, she thought about abandoning her quest, admit she had reached a dead end and move on with her life, the way everyone wanted her to. But another part of her wanted to go on, to dig deeper into the secret her father had taken such great pains to hide.

No matter what he had done, he hadn't deserved death for it.

The cab Cynthia Parson had called for her suddenly appeared and pulled up along the curb.

With a small sigh of disappointment, Jill stepped in and told the driver to take her to National Airport.

It was time to return to New York.

"I've always said, there's nothing more arousing than the sight of a man with an ax in his hands."

At the sound of the sexy female voice, Dan lowered his arms and turned around.

Olivia Bennett stood six feet away. She was as alluring as he remembered. Three years older than Jill, she was anything but the girl next door, and she knew it. Every move she made, every syllable she spoke, every glance that smoldered from beneath those thick black lashes was as strategically calculated as a military battle. To Olivia Bennett, seduction was second nature, as necessary to her as the air she breathed.

"Hello, Olivia."

"That's it? We haven't laid eyes on one another in twelve years and all you can say is hello, Olivia?"

"You look terrific." He smiled. "That's what you wanted to hear, isn't it?"

"It'll do, for now." She made a moue that on anyone else would have looked silly. On her it looked sexy as hell. "I keep forgetting that you're a man of few words."

Setting another log on the old tree stump, Dan gave it a solid whack, splitting it neatly down the middle. "I wasn't aware you knew where my family lived."

"I looked you up in the phone book." She waved

toward the house. "Your mother is amazing. She recognized me right away."

"She has a good eye."

Walking over to the picnic bench, she sat down and crossed her shapely legs. Though her short skirt rode up to the top of her thighs, she made no effort to pull it down. "Why didn't you let me know you were in town? I had to hear it through the grapevine."

Dan split another log. Twelve years ago, when he and Jill had announced they were divorcing, Olivia had let him know that she was available and willing to mend his wounded heart, a gesture he knew stemmed more from a burning desire to have something, or someone, Jill no longer had, than from genuine attraction.

Fortunately for him, rather than continue her pursuit, Olivia had fallen for an Argentinean polo player and had forgotten all about Dan. "What brings you here, Olivia? If I recall, I'm not exactly on your list of favorite people."

She laughed, a low, throaty laugh that was meant to stir lusty thoughts. "Oh, but you are. Just because you rejected me twelve years ago doesn't mean I stopped liking you. On the contrary, it made you an even greater challenge."

He had to hand it to Olivia. She was brutally honest.

"Actually," she continued, "I'm rather insulted. I heard that you were interrogating members of my family as well as B&A employees regarding Simon's death, but you never came to me." She fluttered those dark, lethal eyelashes. "What's the matter, Detective? Aren't I a good enough suspect for you?"